I took another sip and arched an eyebrow at him.

Stabbing was messy but also utilized functional weapons. I had a leather awl near my left arm. All it would take was to casually set my mug down, pick up the tool, and stick it through his damn lazy eye.

"What? You ain't gonna say nothing?"

I set the cup down and touched the awl with my fingertips. My latest project, a soft bleached fawn-colored suede hide, shaved to only a few millimeters thick, was on my lap to save it from Theo's boot filth. The leather was softer than kitten fur, flexible, and took stains like a bitch. Killing him would have to wait.

"When should I warn her about his left hook?"

"Betty Jo, don't be like that. You know men don't like bitter women. You need to be sweeter. Maybe then you'd land a man."

Yes, he went there.

"Sweeter?" I dangled the word out there like fish bait.

Misfit Ink
5257 Buckystown Pike, #215
Frederick, MD 21704
MisfitInkBooks.com

Ordering Information:
For details, contact theAuthor@CaliaWilde.com

Disclaimer:
This book is a work of fiction. Any references to historical events, real people, or real locales are used fictitiously. Other names, characters, places, and incidents are the product of the author's imagination, and any resemblance to actual events or locales or persons, living or dead, is entirely coincidental.

The following is an indication and acknowledgement of potential content that may be upsetting or triggering, but is clearly not exhaustive:

Vulgar language, abuse (physical, sexual, emotional, verbal), sexual assault, suicidal thoughts, excessive or gratuitous violence, kidnapping (forceful deprivation of/disregard for personal autonomy), death or dying, miscarriages, cancer, and blood.

Cover design and publication layout: Misfit Ink Books (MisfitInkBooks.com)

Front cover photography: used under license through Adobe Stock Photography

ALSO BY CALIA WILDE

DESTROYERS SERIES

Motorcycle Club Romance, Contemporary Action/
Adventure Romance Novels and Short Stories

DEVILS HANDMAIDENS MOTORCYCLE CLUB

Motorcycle Club Romance, Contemporary Action/Adventure
Romance Novels — A shared MC universe with other MC authors

DESANTOS TRILOGY

Contemporary Romance/Romantic Suspense

BONES SERIES

Paranormal and Fantasy Romantic Short Stories,
Mythology-inspired Romantic Tales

TKI LOGISTICS

Contemporary Romance, Military Romance Short Stories

Visit https://caliawilde.com/book-backlist/ for
a full list of current publications.

Contents

BIKER QUEEN

A Destroyers MC Throwback Novel

by

Calia Wilde

Misfit Ink Books

Maryland, USA

CHAPTER 1

Stockton, California – about sixteen years before "Down in Blood"

My cousin, Theo, was a certified idiot. Just because he didn't have a piece of paper proclaiming the authenticity of his stupidity, his rap sheet should've sufficed. Then again, he wasn't doing anything different than our family had done for decades, starting with my grandpa, sliding down the branch to his kids, including my pa, and right over to Theo—or "Bear" as he was known to his biker brothers.

Luckily, my pa had some sense and retired from being a full member of the Wicked Legion Motorcycle Club. Instead, he was their mechanic—and a damn good one. Every biker in San Joaquin County knew him as "Wrench," whether they were in a club or not.

That meant our house connected to his repair shop was a second clubhouse where every asshole biker in the area stopped by to drink our beer and fuck with me.

At sixteen, I thought it cute and romanticized that one day I'd marry a biker like my dear old dad.

Knocked up at seventeen wasn't the right way to go about those plans.

Neither was getting hitched to a cheating asshole with aspirations of becoming the chief bastard in charge of the Wicked Legion.

I never got the chance to be a mom. It was bad enough I gained over a hundred pounds from gestational diabetes, but losing about five years to being broken apart over and over again turned my heart against bikers, no matter how great Pa was.

When I was twenty-seven, I moved back into the house attached to the garage and lost three-hundred and ten pounds.

Too bad two-eighty of it was attached to a dick. On second thought, that was a blessing. Roger "Road King" Nelson was a lying bastard who had the nerve to knock up not one but TWO of the club whores during our marriage.

Which circled right back around to the reason Theo was a certified idiot. He didn't have the good sense God gave him to keep his fucking trap shut about my ex. He sat in the easy chair somebody "rescued" from a dumpster with his feet up on the oak desk Pa dumped in the middle of the room. I sat behind it, staring at Theo's heels and pretended to listen.

What I really wanted was to kick him out, shut the door between the two buildings, and lock out any bad memories old Theo dragged out in his soliloquy.

In short, Roger was getting hitched to his going-to-be next baby momma. I didn't hold anything against her for falling for Roger's bullshit, but maybe, just maybe, I didn't want to hear every little fucking detail?

"Pres says she can hook her legs behind her ears."

I sipped my tea and contemplated murder.

"She's got big tits, too. Did I tell you that?" Theo made the motions around his own man-boobs. He'd been going on for at least twenty minutes singing the praises of Jennifer-something—I'd blocked her last name. She was twenty, blonde, perfectly cute, long-legged, and had big tits. If I didn't know better, I'd call bullshit on Theo, dreaming up a Barbie doll instead of a real woman. But then again, Jennifer's description matched the last two women Roger knocked up.

This one wasn't a bike bunny, though, and this time, old Roger was single.

"And her daddy owns a tire store."

I took another sip and arched an eyebrow at him.

Stabbing was messy but also utilized functional weapons. I had a leather awl near my left arm. All it would take was to casually set my mug down, pick up the tool, and stick it through his damn lazy eye.

"What? You ain't gonna say nothing?"

I set the cup down and touched the awl with my fingertips. My latest project, a soft bleached fawn-colored suede hide, shaved to only a few millimeters thick, was on my lap to save it from Theo's boot filth. The leather was softer than kitten fur, flexible, and took stains like a bitch. Killing him would have to wait.

"When should I warn her about his left hook?"

"Betty Jo, don't be like that. You know men don't like bitter women. You need to be sweeter. Maybe then you'd land a man."

Yes, he went there.

"Sweeter?" I dangled the word out there like fish bait.

"Yeah, you know, like Lucy."

AKA Lucy the Loose. The current club whore my cousin Theo, and about a dozen others, were fucking. She smelled like cheap perfume and unwashed underwear. I couldn't see the appeal. Then again, I wasn't a grown man who shirked responsibilities and thought the epitome of machismo was getting bugs splattered into your teeth at sixty miles per hour. Nor was I vying for the attention of any man like that. I'd learned my lesson with Roger. Bikers were bad news. Trouble was, there was no escaping them as long as Pa fixed the things they broke.

I pretended to contemplate Theo's suggestion that I be sweeter.

"Maybe... Should I smile more?"

"Yeah. Smile more. That's a start." He propped his hands on top of his beer gut and wiggled his boots, probably thinking he'd said something profound.

Project or not, I'd have to hide the body. That would take time and planning, and then I'd have to get rid of the five Wicked Legion motorcycle club members in the garage bay who'd see me dragging Theo's corpse out

of the connecting office addition through the parking lot to my tiny Honda.
Shit. He probably wouldn't fit in the back.

Maybe if I dragged him through the house to fertilize the pitiful garden
in the backyard? That would be one way to conceal my crime from prying
eyes. There was still the problem of nosy bikers.

They traveled in packs like hyenas. Eventually, one would trail in trying
to find "Bear." Then the rest would follow. Ugh. Counting Theo, there were
an even half-dozen bikers to deal with. That was too much work to justify
killing my cousin. I opted for insulting him instead.

"Theo, did you know that you have the emotional sensitivity of a goat?"
I smiled widely.

His boots hit the floor. But he was too lazy to stand up and lean over the
desk to intimidate me.

"You're a bitch, Betty Jo. A right bitch."

I'd been called that nasty word several times. So often, it rolled right off
me. I turned my attention to making delicate stitches along the seam of the
halter the leather would someday be. It was slow, tedious work. But I had no
other way of doing it. I couldn't afford a regular sewing machine, let alone
an industrial one for sewing leather. The model I had my eye on cost almost
half a year's work.

I wasn't making enough despite living with Pa and sewing leather
purses and saddle bags when I could. If I had a machine, it'd probably triple
or quadruple my output and pay for itself, but if I didn't have scratch to
start with, scratch wasn't going to find its way to me. I took another stitch
and stuffed my dreams away. They landed on top of my hopes and some
memories that were better left buried.

One day, I'd leave California and things would be better. Maybe
wherever that was, I'd make enough money to take a cruise. There I could
get "stranded" at an island resort and spend my days sipping daiquiris and
ogling the cabana boys—someday.

Oh, the lies you tell yourself. Maybe I was as certifiable as Theo. Did
that sort of thing run in families? *Probably.* None of my uncles or cousins
amounted to anything except the moniker of "notorious felon." Each one

rotten to the core and jumping from one disaster to the next. Darwin weeded them all out until it was only Pa, Theo, and me left.

"Yo, Betty Jo!"

The call came from the garage bay. The caterwauling sounded like Bones, the vice president of the Wicked Legion.

"What?" I screamed to be heard over the sputtering of a misfiring Harley. My head streamed through a list of reasons for that noise, and I shook those thoughts away, knowing I didn't want to be a mechanic like Pa. The first time I'd broken a nail while trying to change a fouled spark plug was enough.

"Those saddle bags done yet?" He stomped in, dragging dirt and grease from the garage into the office where my leather work mingled with Pa's papers.

"I told you, I won't buy the hide until you pay half down."

"I ain't paying half, cuz I ain't payin' nothing. Now get ordering that leather."

He waltzed back out, leaving behind dirt and a puddle of anger churning in my gut. Bones was a great friend of my ex. So much so it was difficult to tell them apart by how they acted. Of course, they looked completely different, so there was that. But both were rotten-ass mother-fuckers who treated me like dirt. They treated Pa like dirt, too. Had been doing that ever since I moved back in with him after the divorce.

I tossed the halter down and stood in the doorway to yell at Bones. But my planned words were cut short because we had a customer. From the quality of his bike, a paying one.

Unfortunately, the six club members circled him like buzzards.

"Hey? Can I help you?"

The stranger rode a sweet Wide Glide that purred like a grumpy tiger. I couldn't hear anything wrong with the machine. This rider wasn't a weekend warrior or a waxer or nothing, and he took good care of his ride. Not to mention, he had an impressive set of riding leathers. The chaps were custom.

I'd know, seeing as making custom chaps was about half my business. They didn't take nearly as long to sew as saddlebags, making them a staple.

"Got a flat kit?" he stood on his toes to yell over the wall of men.

"You ain't buying anything here." Bones leaned so close he practically touched the guy's bike—an insult if there ever was one.

"Bullshit he ain't." I grabbed the nearest kit. We had a stock of a dozen or more on hand. I trotted over to the cluster of men. I shoved my cousin out of the way to hand it over. "Thirty bucks."

Bones plucked it right out of my hands. "I said, he ain't buying it here. Go fuck yourself, Destroyer."

Oh, shit. The Destroyers Motorcycle Club was the enemy. I couldn't see the back of his coat from where I'd been, but up close, it was clear this man wasn't a person to be fucked with.

He pulled out a huge revolver from under his vest and pointed it at Bones' nose. "You're lucky I'm letting you live and not killing you on sight."

Without taking his eyes off Bones, he pulled a fifty-dollar bill out of a pocket and stretched his arm out toward me. "For the kit."

I grabbed the kit from Bones, who was frozen more solid than my heart, and pushed it into the biker's hands. The money got fumbled in the exchange and blew into the bay. As I scrambled after it, a shot rang out.

After years of built-up reflexes, I hit the dirty floor and scrambled for the nearest workbench to hide under. Trouble was, there were parts and other shit in my way. I bumped into at least two sharp edges and one really hard piece of iron that knocked my kneecap into the I-wanna-scream-it-hurts-so-bad zone.

The biker tore off, and I poked my head up to see who was bleeding.

Surprisingly, no one was.

"Where'd that bullet go?" I asked, wondering how the heck things had escalated so quickly.

Theo pointed at the roof.

Sure as shit, sunlight streamed through a neat hole a little bigger than my finger.

"Wow." Pa was going to have to get that fixed.

"Bones, you got some kind of balls to push his gun up like that." Coyote led the ass-kissing section. The Wicked Legion's VP almost bit the dirt today, which had to ruffle his feathers a bit. So, he was eating the praise up, puffing his chest out like a peacock, and swaggering in place.

Theo added his two cents. "Did you see his patch? Enforcer. D'ya think it was from the club across the border?"

"Naw," Bones spit on the floor, "the bottom rocker said *nomad*." He sent the street the hairy eyeball while trying to act nonchalant about almost getting shot in the nose.

I swallowed the lump in my throat. Being around the life for as long as I'd been, I knew what all that meant. First, the nearest Destroyers were in Nevada. California was a no-go zone for them. Other clubs, including the Wicked Legion, scrabbled for territory in the state, each bowing to the ruling club, which was the Destroyers' main nemesis. The man shouldn't have put a front wheel across the border, let alone ride almost to the center of the state. That was a terrific way to start a war.

Second, Nomads do two things. Mostly, they mind their own business and keep a low profile. It's when they don't that things get ugly.

The simple and short story was that Pa's shop had been targeted as a weak point if a nomad was in the area and showed up here. Perhaps he was only scouting territory under the premise of buying a flat repair kit, seeing as they were right there in plain view.

Or he was testing the Wicked Legion's resolve. Destroyers had a "shoot on sight" rule for some MCs. The Wicked Legion were on that list. Sure, there was supposed to be a truce going on, but that never stopped the violence for long. There were a million reasons why, none of them good.

It didn't matter the reason; trouble was coming.

"What the fuck were you thinking, selling that Destroyer the kit? Don't you know he's the enemy?"

Theo's voice droned into the background, complaints and grumbles I was quick to tune out. Only Bones' voice made it through.

"It's a damn good thing Prez still has a soft spot for you. Otherwise, I'd shoot you myself."

A tear dripped down my cheek. I didn't bother wiping it away because that could draw attention to it. I faced the wall. No one needed to know how badly Bones' words dug in. I picked up the fifty where it had gotten trapped near the tire machine, then bee-lined for the office.

I hated being weak. Worse, I hated being weak in front of my ex's gang. If Roger still had a soft spot for me, I wasn't going to give anyone the satisfaction of knowing that the soft spot I had for him was encased in an iron box, then wrapped with two tons' worth of proverbial ice queen personality that made everyone call me a bitch. I'd armored myself with it to hide how hard that damned soft spot hurt.

To bury their suspicion, I slammed the door as hard as possible.

My shaking hands were a dead giveaway that my emotions had gone haywire. I stuffed the fifty into the safe slot.

Theo burst into the office, followed by Bones. "What the fuck do you mean we ain't giving it back?" My cousin then snapped his fingers at me. "Hand it over, Betty Jo. That's club money."

"Too late." I pointed at the safe.

"Bitch—" Theo's voice was drowned out by Bones'.

"Forget the money. Get your bike. I'm calling church. Get the rest of the motherfuckers together and start calling down the line." He turned to me, "You didn't see or hear nothing, got it?"

"What didn't I see or hear?" I snapped back. Sometimes, I forgot my place. MCs had all sorts of strange rules, from benign ones like calling meetings "church" to nasty ones that treated women like property rather than human beings.

Bones' eyes narrowed. "You didn't hear what we were talking about from the time that asshole rode up to right now, got it?" His tone meant he was dead serious.

I tipped my head and put on my sweetest voice. It worked on Roger sometimes. Maybe Bones wasn't immune. "You came in here bitching about your saddlebags, then some idiot drove up and shot up the place. Will that do?"

His right eyebrow inched up a fraction higher than the other one. "And after?"

Maybe I could make this worth my headache?

"And after he got gone, I bitched at you about the price of leather going up. Two-hundred-and-fifty is fair, no?"

"One hundred," he countered.

"That won't cover it." I tapped my lips to remind him he was buying my silence as well as the fucking hide.

"And you get to keep that fucking fifty, okay?"

"Deal. I'm quite honestly confused why anyone would be upset with you, Bones. Guy must have been an asshole with a death wish. Too bad I didn't hear nothing." I wiggled my fingers at him to hand over the hundred.

He dug into his wallet and passed it over. I made a show of taking the money and stuffing it between my boobs. His eyes followed the action and lingered there. Then they met mine.

If almost getting shot didn't scare me, the chill in his eyes did.

CHAPTER 2

"I don't give a shit where you stick it, just don't leave it there."

Big Mike was in rare form. We went way back to my prospect days when he was still a regular asshole, not the killer he'd become. I hadn't seen him in over two long-ass years, and before he even said, "Hi, Fin, how's it hanging?" He was on his fucking phone screaming at some idiot.

I guess being the strong left hook for the national Destroyers president came with a bunch of headaches, which was why I was doubly grateful to be away from all the bullshit.

While he reamed someone a new asshole, I secured the forge door and straightened my tools and hammers. Ant and I ran a metal working business out of an old farm spread in the middle of the San Joaquin Valley. The work consisted mostly of farm machinery repairs, rebuilding pieces you could no longer buy, and some blacksmithing on the side. The really interesting work came with the traveling fairs we attended each summer. For them, we built swords, knives, and anything intricate or pointy. It all sold like hotcakes, and kept us busy when things got lean. He'd been in the business his whole life. Me? I'd been immersed in it almost since I met Ant. He was a good friend and a fellow Destroyer. I pledged my life to the club because of him. And, when Ant set out on his own, I eventually followed because someone needed to watch over him. Otherwise, he'd have been dead long ago.

My mentor was getting up there in years. Taking care of him was almost a full-time job in itself. Any free time I had beyond that was eaten up trying to keep my tattoo parlor open. It didn't give me much time for fun.

But who needed fun? Not me. I'd had my fill of chasing skirt and killing my liver. The last bitch I'd poked a stick at stole practically everything I had. She even tried to steal my bike.

Any woman who does that doesn't deserve a second chance. No matter how sweet their pussy tastes.

Big Mike snapped the phone shut with a flick of his wrist and scrubbed his hand through his thinning hair. "Fucking idiots."

"Do I need to fire up the chimney?" The chimney was a medium-sized coke forge Ant and I used for the large works. It got up to over three thousand degrees and reduced fillings and bones to powder much quicker than most methods. Heck, it worked faster than a crematorium, which was why I could be happily living the Nomad life smack dab in the middle of enemy territory. My role was useful, quiet, and discreet in ways that couldn't be traced. No one called attention to us—which was the way I liked it. I never wanted fame, just peace and a well-tuned motorcycle.

He knew what I was asking. Big Mike and I did some dirty shit for the club back in the day. We'd gotten a reputation for it. While his M.O. was more hammer than finesse, both of us got the job done. Or used to. Lately, I longed for a quiet life. One where any involvement in the workings of the Destroyers was at my whim, not theirs. Big Mike showing up made the hairs on the back of my neck crawl. What was worse, he hadn't outright said what he needed. That boded ill for me. Whatever he was involved in this time was complicated. I hated that word—complicated.

"Naw, they're just assholes. Picked up a fucking truck on the border by Tahoe, and it's packed to the rim with stolen parts. But they didn't think ahead far enough to figure out where to hide a whole goddamn truckload of crap."

"Are there serial numbers on the parts?"

"Yup. All fucking registered."

"Then, how do you know they're stolen?"

Big Mike lifted his head from the disgusted grumbling he was doing to tell me straight. "Ours."

"The fuck?" My mouth worked faster than my thoughts. But those were catching up fast. If we'd stolen back stolen parts... the possibilities for those mother-fucking complications grew exponentially.

"Yep. That's right. I can see your gears turning. Those parts were last seen in Gary, Indiana, and suddenly they're being transported from Cali into Nevada."

That prickle turned into a full-blown headache at the base of my skull. "Who was moving them?"

"Who do you think? Same dickheads we've been at war with for-fucking-ever."

Ah. That was a problem too close to home. Mike's visit here wasn't random. The local boys, going by the idiotic name of "Wicked Legion," were another reason I maintained a low profile. I'd kept my name out of their mouths for four long years. Any escalation between the clubs meant our home could and would be a target.

Worse, Ant's farm wasn't exactly fortified. Sure, there were farms surrounding the area for miles, but every few acres, dirt roads connected the fields providing access to the irrigation systems. Truckloads of migrant workers traveled those roads daily for as long as the sun shone and the crops grew.

It wouldn't take much for the enemy to pick us as their target for retaliation since we were technically trespassing. Not that any Destroyer gave a shit what other clubs thought—I sure as hell didn't unless that thought was pointed at me.

"Do you think it's going to escalate?"

Big Mike scowled. "Already has."

I set my favorite hammer down carefully. "How?"

"Was on a little look-see ride. Stopped at their garage, you know... that run-down bike shop off Milton?" He snapped his fingers, trying to remember and coming up empty.

I nodded; I knew the place and knew enough about it to steer well clear.

Heck, I avoided the Wicked Legion's turf as much as possible. Even my tattoo shop was as far from their stomping grounds as possible. It tucked into a little strip of buildings off the highway that snaked through Valley Springs. I didn't make much from it, but I had a chair, a loyal clientele, and solid bars on the windows, so it wasn't messed with. It didn't hurt that I was a favorite supplier of forged steel to the gun shop next door. He bought all sorts of stuff from Ant and I. But mostly, his customers loved my knives. I was backlogged for a full year with custom work. From pocket-sized folding blades and little Kiridashi daggers up to hunting knives and fully functional swords, I made 'em and stamped my mark on them. That shark fin rising up from the wave touch mark meant something to collectors.

When I lit the "open" sign, it was guaranteed at least one or two walk-ins would migrate from next door with their minds set on talking my ear off about how much they liked their new knife—that or what they wanted next. Sometimes, they'd get a tattoo. And that meant another loyal customer. While my knives were premium work, my tattoos were apex. Any Destroyer worth his salt came to me. Any non-Destroyer was lucky to have my marks on 'em.

"Ain't you gonna ask what happened?" Big Mike stood there with his fists on his hips.

"Figured I'd let you talk."

"That's what I like about you, Fin. You don't interrupt. So, as I was sayin', did a little recon." He paused with a look on his face like I was supposed to encourage him or something. When I didn't, his mouth twisted down. "And those bastard Wicked Legion were there. A full half-dozen of 'em."

That was about all of the club members. They hadn't done much recruiting recently, their total number without prospects was around ten. Their president was a lazy fuck. Ten wasn't nearly enough for a club.

Then again, that was perfect for me because it meant they weren't poking around Ant's spread or my shop.

"Asshole VP of theirs got in my face, and I had to pull my gun."

That got my attention. "Ya kill him?" Killing someone would make things a bit more urgent.

"Fucker knocked my hand before I could plant a bullet between his eyes."

Well. Ol' Bones had moves. That was worth knowing. A missed shot wasn't as much of a problem as a dead brother. My relief leaked out as I waited for Mike to expand on his story. He loved an audience. Since I was privy to his secrets and didn't talk much, we made a good match.

"Almost hit the girl running the place." The lines between his eyebrows puckered up in concern.

I shook my head. Big Mike had a soft spot for ladies. Any lady. Didn't matter if she was five or fifty. His big old heart would turn to mush. That was deadly for a man in his position.

"One of these days, a woman is going to get you in trouble," I pointed out.

"Speaking of, you still seeing that redhead?"

My nostrils flared and my jaw tightened. Thank God he hadn't spoken her name. I don't think I would have been able to keep my shit together if he had. "Nope."

His eyebrow shot up. "Why not?"

"She's a bitch." A lying, cheating, thieving bitch. Don't get me wrong, I love a woman who knows their mind and doesn't shy away from telling it, but there is an enormous difference between that and dragging a man down because you can. It was a lesson I'd learned in the worst way possible. One I intended never to repeat.

Big Mike shook his head. "Here I thought you'd be settling down the way you were going on and on about her last I saw you."

"That was two years ago. Things change."

"Do they?" He looked around the barn Ant and I used as a smithy. "Cuz this place hasn't changed one bit."

"It's the way we like it." He needed to get to the point of his visit because all this chit-chat grew irritating.

"You're going to die alone, Finnigan Curty." His fat finger pointed at me.

"Beats dying around people. That'd be embarrassing."

His guffaws rang off the rafters. "You're a hoot." He slapped his thigh and let the fits of laughter settle before getting serious with me again. "You up for a ride along?" Finally, he was getting to the point.

"Now?" I was working on a custom piece for the festival next month. It could wait, but I hated leaving a piece at mid-creation.

"Naw, Saturday. Saw a sign at the shop for a swap meet. I wanna check to see if any more of our shit is there since I couldn't talk to the owner today. I have a feeling there'll be more. And if there is, and those bastard Wicked Legion are there, I'll need backup."

"You'll need more than that." A swap meet meant full club attendance. While ten Wicked Legion weren't many, ten against two was not good odds.

"Thinking maybe we'll get a couple of prospects from Gardnerville and their enforcers to come along. You think Ant will be interested?"

Nope. Well, he'd be interested but not able. Ant wasn't up to much lately. Chemo sucked the light out of him. "He's busy."

Big Mike frowned. "Too busy to back up a brother?" His voice took that tone I would generally avoid.

"Cancer, or didn't you hear?"

His face paled. "Aw, man, sorry. I didn't know." His tone softened. Normally, I'd take offense at it because sentimentality wasn't my thing, except when it came to Ant.

Ant was more than my boss. When I was growing up, my pops would beat the shit out of me. One September, I was at a county fair, and he pulled that shit in front of where Ant had set up an old-fashioned shoeing demonstration in the horse barn. Despite not being as big as my father, Ant picked up his hammer and threatened to pound my old man's skull in.

It was the first time anyone had stuck up for me.

I paid attention to that. And when I ran away from home a couple years later, I looked him up. Ol' Ant set me up doing the grunt work for his blacksmithing business. On weekends, he'd let me tag along to pig roasts, and sometimes I'd get to ride in the chaser van during club events. That's how I'd met Big Mike and the local Destroyers. From that point on, I lived and died with bikes and hammers. Tattooing grew out of my love of doodling, and I had a real knack for it. It had taken a few years to learn, but I took to it much faster than I did smithing.

A decade back, Ant's old man, a pisser like mine, kicked the bucket and deeded him a bunch of valley dirt. The homestead that had been in their family since a great-grandpappy moved from Minnesota to California for the Gold Rush came with it, along with all of the buildings. The new barn had more than enough room for a decent forge, and there was passive income leasing the fields to the produce companies who always needed land. Ant was set up well.

But Ant being Ant, he pissed away most of it on booze and smoke. Things got rough for a bit. Every visit, he seemed worse than before. I decided that a good brother, and a good friend, needed to step in. But that meant leaving my chapter behind. I didn't like change; however, there wasn't much choice in the matter.

Turning Nomad so I could follow Ant to the San Joaquin Valley was the best decision I ever made. Winters were brutal in Minnesota.

Old Ant was like a father to me. Knowing he was dying had sunk its boney fingers into my heart and made me bitter. I beat the pain out on horseshoes and knives.

But a man can't live solely on pain. Getting out for a day with Big Mike was the balm I needed to remember there was a whole brotherhood out there I could rely on.

"No big. Hell, maybe I'll find me a new girlfriend while we're there." I smiled at my joke. No woman in their right mind would want me. I brushed my fingers down my beard. It had been years since I'd shaved. My best clothes were my cut and my boots. I wasn't into buying jewelry when I could make it myself. Nor was I big on conversation.

Frankly, I was lucky to have gotten laid at all, which was probably why I'd put up with so much shit for as long as I had.

"That's the spirit!" Mike slapped my back and began making plans.

Two days later, those plans went to hell. Mike gathered four others to join on his little ride along. Tiktock and Dirtball were enforcers. Good men to have at our sides. The other two I was iffy on. Prospects barely old enough to shave. Don't remember their names.

"Chicago wants a war," Mike pointed out.

I listened to the Gardnerville crew yap while we walked from the parking lot into the fairgrounds. The mid-day California sun beat down on us, causing sweat to collect under my arms. We were running sixty-six, or without colors, but we did wear leather riding gear.

Dirtball matched his pace to Big Mike's and got starry-eyed at Mike's talk of war. "We can get twenty riders up from Henderson and another fifteen over from Frisco. I hear there's even a dozen down the coast near L.A."

While the valley and points south toward Los Angeles were clearly not Destroyers' territory, we'd made inroads. There were a half-dozen satellite chapters begging for Destroyers charters, and the entire valley was a mess of gangs who owed no one loyalty but hated the fuck out of our enemies. That was damn useful. Trouble was, we hadn't done enough to cultivate their friendship. Some Destroyers even went as far as being assholes toward the Mexican clubs, so I highly doubted we would win a war in this state if there was one.

I chewed on my lip to keep my thoughts inside.

"How strong is the local club?" Tictock asked. His question was aimed at me, so I had to answer it.

"Don't know for certain. But they didn't chase Big Mike down after he shot at 'em, so can't say they are ready for a war." Trouble was, they were a sight more ready than we were because they had the home-field advantage.

"See? Fin's got all sorts of stuff in his head that's useful." Big Mike laughed and slapped me on the back. His grin dropped faster than a lead pellet. "But he's right to be cautious. Their second-in-command has got balls."

"We need someone on the inside," Dirtball noted.

"A prospect." Tictock scanned the lot for threats.

"Or one of their club-whores." Big Mike stopped, thinking harder. "Find one that's jilted and ready to flip."

"Shouldn't be hard. They're all ugly assholes." I was talking to myself more than to the crew. Should have kept my mouth shut.

"Like you, Fin?" The taunt fired back quickly.

"Fuck off." I strode on ahead, not willing to be the brunt of some pretty boy's jokes. Tictock was still a pup.

There were tents and vendors set up, but I was on a beeline to the beer tent. If there was trouble, that would be where it would be. And, if there were Wicked Legion here, they'd be there as well.

I was itching for a fight.

"Yo, Fin, grab me a beer." Big Mike's words boomed over the crowd.

"I ain't your bitch!" I yelled back, turning half around and whipping him the bird. I walked about three steps, not minding where I was going, before being stopped abruptly by something soft and solid.

"Watch where the fuck you're walking, you dick!"

She had the mouth of a sailor, the curves of a Venus, and the face of a wicked angel. I was smitten. Her hair was blacker than raven feathers, her lips more luscious than ripe cherries, and her eyes—my god, a man could fall into them and drown.

Not to mention, she had an ass that wouldn't quit. I could hammer at it and happily lose myself forever. My fingers lingered where they'd landed as I steadied her. She was a handful.

Naw, more than a handful—a fucking goddess.

"Where have you been hiding my entire life?" My brain was obviously not running the conversation. If it had, I would have said something better.

CHAPTER 3

"You can't tell me that lame-ass line works."

The man who bumped into me as I stood in line hadn't moved his hands. The poor wretch looked smitten. I felt sorry for him but also kind of flattered.

Okay, more than kind of. Hella flattered. Not once had anyone looked at me like that. Not even 'Roger the Philanderer' had given me such a smoldering gaze. And my ex knew how to turn up the heat. But in hindsight, there was always something superficial about it. He didn't look at me like I was the sun. This man did.

My heartbeat fluttered faster, drowning out the noise of the crowd and my head.

He wasn't bad-looking for a biker. His beard would have to go, but his eyes were interesting, somewhere between light green and hazel. Piercingly sharp and intelligent. They reminded me of a gunslinger I'd seen in a movie. I didn't know the actor's name, just that he was the villain. That always got my heart skipping all pitter-patter. Give me the bad guy any day, especially if they were bad for a reason. Rogues, cutthroats, fighters, they were catnip. Someone so independent that they didn't answer to anyone. I'd grown up around that sort. Learned that even under all that grime and grit, sometimes there was a heart of gold buried. My father was one of those. He'd loved my mother hard and never remarried. Took care of me like I was a princess when she lit out, not being able to handle the very things that I craved.

But there were assholes in those circles.

As I stood there, lost in this man's eyes, I hoped like hell I hadn't found another one of those. But his eyes looked honest. They were catlike in shape with little white lines at the outer edges where the sun didn't tan the skin. They were the kind of eyes that spoke volumes. If you were in his sights, you'd be dead. Yet, I wasn't afraid. Hell no. I was turned on.

He closed his mouth and swallowed. "No, can't say it should."

What were we talking about? Right. Lame pickup lines.

His fingers tightened for a fraction of a second and then released like I was molten lava or something. He brushed his hands against his ass, where the chaps he wore gave way to faded jeans.

I let out a breath because even from the front, he cut an impressive figure. Wide shoulders, muscular arms, narrow waist, and a bulge.

We're talking capital B, curving nicely to the right.

"Excuse me." He tipped his head at me like he was a gentleman or something, then walked into the crowd of thirsty drunks surrounding the beer tent.

His ass was as fine as that bulge.

I ached to get my hands on him.

"Where's my plate, woman?"

"Fuck off with that shit, Theo." I pushed my cousin, who'd caught me gaping.

The commotion caught my stranger's attention. His sharp gaze bounced between Theo and I and back again. Then his eyebrows came down in a scowl. His frown followed.

So much for making a good impression.

I shoved Theo again on principle. "Get out of my way. I need to get back to the tent." As much as I'd love to grab a beer and flirt with a total stranger, I had more important things to do than guzzle carbs and court embarrassment.

"Who is that guy?"

"What guy?" I played dumb.

"The biker." Theo's eyes narrowed when he saw someone walk up and slap my future shame on the back.

I followed his glare.

"Oh shit." The newcomer was the same biker who shot a hole in Pa's roof.

"Fucking Destroyers. I'll kill 'em." His hands fisted, and he took a step. I stopped him because as much as I hated my cousin, he was my cousin, and I didn't want to see him dead.

"There's six of them."

And maybe more. Bikers traveled in hordes.

Standing with he-who-I-shouldn't-be-attracted-to, there were two burly men, both nearing fifty, or maybe beyond if the thinning hair and gray that flirted around their ears was any indication, a young buck in his prime, and two prospects. I knew this because they had that look—the one that's all puppy-eyed, expectant, wary, and if they had a tail, it would wag any time they glanced at their handlers—just before they bared their teeth. In other words, a couple of useful idiots who'd eventually become useful asshole idiots.

"Gonna get Roger." Theo took off. I pinched the narrow space just above my nose, where a headache bloomed. The heat, lack of food, the noise, and knowing there was going to be bloodshed made it grow into a migraine. That was the last thing I needed today.

I stumbled back to the tent Pa set up with the bike parts we were selling at the meet. My space was off to the side. I'd arrayed a few smaller items on the table, and there were two wardrobe racks with leather chaps, vests, belts, and halters hung up behind them.

A lonely metal folding chair waited at the end of the table. I collapsed into it, fanning myself.

"Told you not to overdo it." Pa handed me a bottle of water.

"I'm good." The slimy trickle of sweat on the back of my neck told a different story. "There are Destroyers here. At least six of them."

My father needed the warning. While he wasn't club anymore, that didn't mean he wasn't roped into their shit.

"Trouble?"

I stopped rolling the cold bottle against my forehead to shoot him my best "Ya think?" squint.

"Did you eat anything today?"

"I ate." I put the bottle on my neck before cracking it open.

"Then why are you flushed?"

"Because it's hot, damn it."

"Doc said you can't starve yourself."

"For the last time, I am not starving myself. I'm eating healthy."

"Ain't healthy if you are getting sick again."

I sighed. He meant well, but he didn't have a clue. "I'll eat."

"No rabbit food."

My hand shot out to indicate the tents. "Do you realize where we are? There isn't a bit of lettuce nearby for at least a mile."

Pa, just to be contrary, tipped his head toward the fields. Sure as shit, it was leafy and green.

"I stand corrected."

His sharp nod marked his victory. "Destroyers, you say? Were they wearing color?"

"No."

"Then how'd you know?"

"Because one of them is the same guy who shot a hole in your roof."

"Huh. Okay."

He straightened a bin of parts and set a few pieces on the table.

I gaped at him. For being a former member and a lifetime biker, he wasn't giving much mind to the shit storm about to erupt.

"That's it? That's all the reaction you're going to give?"

"It's a public meet. They ain't wearing colors. Nothing we can do about it."

I blinked twice.

"But Theo—"

"Your no-good cousin starts busting heads and gets his ass arrested means nothing to us."

He didn't look at me, so I knew something else was up.

"What ain't you telling me?"

"Nothing. Sell your fancy leather and forget about the Destroyers. Got it?"

I wanted to argue with him more, but a cluster of customers came up to our tent and began browsing the merchandise. The women broke off and asked me questions about the halters. I showed a couple off, and while doing that, the crowd attracted more customers. It was strange how that worked. You could sit for hours without a soul to talk to, but get one brave lookie-loo and suddenly there are more folks than you can handle. I'd rather lose a few customers being too busy than watch potential customers walk on by.

Which is why I didn't notice him—my villain-shame man.

But I heard his voice, and my heart sped up. My stomach had honest-to-god butterflies. I glanced around to make certain there weren't any Wicked Legion nearby.

"Hey, beautiful." His voice was smoke brushing softly over gravel, with a lingering sweet note of sex mingled in. Damn. It drove me crazy.

But I pretended to ignore him.

"What's your name? Let me guess—Rose because you're as pretty as one."

I held my breath. Still trying to fight against the effects of his flirting.

"Is that line better?"

"Worse." I laughed because, damn him, he was trying.

He held out a hand. "Finnigan Curty. Everyone calls me Fin."

I took it and admired the strength and the callouses. I hated men with soft hands. Those types made other folks do their dirty work. "Betty Jo."

"Nice to meet you, Betty Jo. I meant it when I said you're beautiful."

"Now that's a much better line."

He smiled. His eye tooth was crooked, and he had a tiny chip in the front. Yet, he was genuine. His face lit up with warmth even as I noticed the flaws. "Good to know. Did you make these?" He pointed at the rack of chaps.

"I did."

His eyebrows went up. "I'm impressed." He moved closer and examined the stitching. "Hand sewn? Holy shit, woman, I've never seen work like this. What else you got?"

The praise was so rare it pierced my heart like a dagger. All the times I'd been ridiculed and all the hours I ignored Theo and the others bugging me about my silly hobby had piled up, and one single line of praise made my emotions come flooding out. My eyes filled up, and I blinked quickly to keep from crying. Once I knew I could control my voice, I spoke, "I got a set of saddlebags I'm working on."

I don't know why I told him that. Technically, they were the ones I made for Bones, but he hadn't paid me for. I'd lied about not being able to buy the leather. I'd already bought it and finished the work, ignoring a few other paying gigs. That's what was making things tight around the shop and was the real reason I'd scrambled across the floor for a fucking fifty-dollar bill.

"Yeah? Lemme see, please?"

Sexy, rugged, and polite. Be still my heart!

I tugged them out and set the finished set on top of the folding table.

Fin inspected the work. "These are real good. Hey, Mike, they'd fit your Dyna," he called to the man who was currently talking to my father. The same one who shot a hole in Pa's garage. The thought crossed my mind to warn my father, but as he reminded me, this was a public place. They were customers, not the enemy.

"Give me a minute. He says they got a part for that XR750."

Fin frowned. "Does he now?" He glanced at me. "Mike's been looking for that for a while."

"What year?" I asked, trying to remember the last inventory list.

"You know bikes?"

"I know some. I'm his daughter." I indicated my father with a tip of my head.

Fin licked his bottom lip. His beard moved with the action, causing it to stick out for a moment. He ran a hand down the length and opened his mouth to say something but was interrupted by the guy he called Mike.

"Let's see." Unlike Fin, Mike's face was easy to read. I knew the second he recognized me. I also saw the way he hesitated and then pretended to play stupid.

In the meantime, Fin pointed out the stitching and the quality of the piece. "You can't find work like this anywhere."

Quietly, I let the happy feeling sink in. I savored it and let it fill me up.

"Do you know parts?" Mike asked.

"I order 'em, sell 'em, but mostly that's Pa's business. This is mine." I gestured to the leather around me.

His eyes shifted from cold to warm. Funny how that sent a shiver down my spine—and not in a good way.

"I'm sure you're great at both." He elbowed Fin and flat out panto-mimed a "do you like what you see?" at Fin.

In response, Fin gave sent him an icy side-eye. "Buy the fucking leather. Then let's go."

"You're helping, remember?"

"And I am. Buy it." Fin tapped the saddle bags. Somehow, I was certain they weren't talking about my creation at all. There was more going on.

"That hole you put in Pa's roof sets the price at double."

The corner of Fin's mouth went up.

Mike noticed. "Ya think this is funny?"

"Hell yeah. What's the price without the ventilation markup?"

"Two-fifty," I lied. Since Bones was getting them for a measly one-fifty, I might as well try for what they were really worth.

"Five big. A fair price for hand-stitched. Don't you think so, Mike?"

His buddy's face soured. Then he did something odd. He turned to Fin and said, "You owe me now. And I know just how you're going to pay me back." Mike slapped five bills into Fin's hand and strode off to talk to my father, leaving us alone.

Fin's skin turned red, and he handed me the five hundred without saying a word.

I offered to write a receipt, but he shook his head.

Just as things got awkward, he blurted out, "You wanna grab something to eat?"

Then he got redder.

It was cute. I bit my lip to keep from laughing. I didn't want to let my joy bubble out and make him think I was mocking him. "I'd love to."

"Make him buy you a damn burger," Pa yelled across the tent. He was in the middle of an exchange with a customer, yet still had eavesdropped on our awkward conversation.

I tucked the money away while Fin hefted the bags over one shoulder. Then, I let him lead me through the crowd. He didn't talk much, and I was too scared we'd bump into Theo or Bones as I scanned the crowd to fill in the conversational holes. But I did finally notice that we weren't heading to the food vendors.

"The burgers are that way." I pointed in the opposite direction.

"Gonna drop these off at the van. Are you okay with that?"

"Sure." I shook my head because why wouldn't I?

He halted in his tracks and stared at me.

"What?"

"Are you naive?"

"No."

"Sheltered?"

I crossed my arms, which caused my tits to squish upward. His eyes got hung up on them. He swallowed twice before he realized he was snared. The light hit his eyes, pulling out the green a bit more.

"I guess not," he said.

"Why did you ask that?"

We started walking again. He scanned the crowd. It was much thinner here, away from the string of tents and food vendors. We got to the parking lot, where he stopped at an old Econoline. He unlocked it, tucked the bags inside, and locked the doors. Only when he was done and he'd steered me back toward the food did he answer.

"I didn't want to freak you out back there."

"Well, you did. Does it always take you that long to answer a simple question?"

"When it's important, and it's for someone important, yeah."

It was my turn to stop and gape at him. "Someone important?"

"You." He did that head-tip thing again.

"I'm not important," I scoffed.

"To me, you are, or could be."

My mouth dropped open. "Are you serious?"

"Most of the time."

I was so confused. I trotted after him, catching up and losing my breath. "Why did you think I was naive?"

"Because you followed a man you didn't know out to his vehicle." Fin turned toward the taco vendor rather than the burger place. I hadn't noticed until we were right in front of it.

"You… you…"

"I was being careful with you."

Oh. Okay. That was sweet. I glanced up at the menu board. My mouth watered. I loved the deep-fried fish tacos but ordered the chicken instead. Food in hand, he steered me toward a stand of trees that cast a nice shady patch on the ground. There was a bushy buckeye that blocked the noise, and the breeze was mild.

As we ate, I found out Fin owned a tattoo shop. And that he was originally from Minnesota. He told me about his childhood, snow, and little things. I grew up right here, so I was fascinated by his tales. Or maybe it was the way he smiled softly or how he knew so much about things. It wasn't just bikes and leather but art, native culture, and food. It was easy to talk to him, and I forgot about my father, my cousin, and the Wicked Legion for a bit.

He broke off a piece of flaky fish and held it out.

One piece couldn't hurt? I let him feed it to me, moaning at the explosion of crusty breading and the delicate flavor of the fish that melted on my tongue. "I miss that flavor."

He'd broken off another piece and froze. "What do you mean?"

I blinked, mortified. "I'm not supposed to have too many fatty foods." I gestured at my stomach and thighs.

He looked me up and down, then shook his head. "You should eat what makes you happy." His tone held a bit of anger in it.

"I'm at high risk of type two diabetes. I have to be careful."

His scowl cleared, and he looked away. "Sorry. I didn't… I mean, shit. Sorry." He set the piece of fish down and wiped his hands.

I picked it up and ate it. "A little bit of happy is worth it, don't you think?"

"Worth every bit as long as it doesn't kill you, okay?" His eyes were guarded, and he kept his head tilted down as if ashamed of himself.

"It won't, I promise." I reached out and patted his arm.

His eyes lit up, and the corners of them crinkled with happiness. I smiled back because it was a sight to behold. A little voice at the back of my head whispered, *"He doesn't get enough of these happy moments, and you just witnessed something special."*

In the little bubble of our smiles, I had the strongest urge to lean in and kiss him. His eyes lingered on my lips in a palpable, hungry way.

But he glanced away at the last minute. "I best get you back. Your pa has got to be wondering if I kidnapped you or something."

"Oh fuck, you're right." I'd forgotten everything. The Wicked Legion, bullet holes, asshole cousins, my work— all of it. This wasn't real. It wouldn't fit with my life. Hell, I could get Fin killed just by having lunch with him. My poor hopeful heart was crushed.

I scrambled to pick up the napkins and wipe the grass from my clothes so it wouldn't look like I'd been rolling around in it.

Fin's chuckle caused me to look over and check on him.

"I like you, Betty Jo."

A little bit of happy was worth the risk, even if he was the enemy.

"I like you, too, Fin."

CHAPTER 4

*D*amn. When Big Mike nudged me to talk to Betty Jo, I didn't expect to like it so much. I mean, yeah, she was attractive as hell. She knew how to enhance her good qualities with makeup and the right clothes. And her curves made my palms itch. But the more I talked and listened, the more I got a peek at the gorgeous woman underneath it all.

Let me tell you, paint is good. It enhanced the pretty face underneath it. Soft skin was great, but a woman who wasn't afraid to talk to a man about real things, that right there was worth gold. I didn't even have to try to carry the conversation. Betty Jo picked up the threads and dragged me along for a pleasant ride. I forgot all about pumping her for information on the Wicked Legion and got caught up in the sunshine and light that was her.

Until I realized I'd fucked around long enough. That almost-kiss was a wake-up call. We were enemies. Hell, I was her enemy, even if she wasn't mine. The whole pretense of this conversation started because Big Mike nudged me in her direction. Any other swap meet, in any other circumstances, I'd have ditched my brothers and wrapped myself in all things Betty Jo. But not at this one. Not with her.

If it were up to me, I'd gladly spend the day with this woman. Hell, I might even consider spending a lifetime with her. She was funny, sweet, honest, and real. Those things were what counted.

But Big Mike needed info.

The shipment of parts caught at the state line wasn't a fluke. In the short time browsing today, we'd uncovered that much. Betty Jo's father had our stolen shit all over the tent. I'd matched IDs on two pieces I picked up, and Big Mike found more. He'd signaled me to talk up Betty Jo while he worked on getting info from the old man. Divide and conquer was the game.

Except it wasn't a game.

This was bullshit. I smelled a rat. This was more than getting sloppy with a shipment. I couldn't put my finger on it yet, but things were off. The timing, or the convenience of finding the parts so easily, or something… it hung there like a thread just waiting to be tugged. Once that action was done, the whole thing would unravel. Or not.

I couldn't discount anything. Chicago wanted a war. Was this a setup? Did they send Big Mike out west to stir shit up? He was a wrecking ball but also damn good at evading responsibility. The best sort of man to send into enemy territory if you wanted chaos.

There'd been a truce for the last two years ever since things when south in the Midwest. Over forty members between the two clubs were locked up because of the violence that our war caused. Knocking heads is one thing. Getting busted for it was a completely other thing. Wars got messy.

Don't get me wrong, if I had to, I'd go down for the club. They'd not steered me wrong, ever. And I owed my entire life to them. It wasn't only because Ant took me in. There was much more to it. I couldn't count how much money I'd made off of club members from tattoos. Nor could I put a price tag on the things I'd learned.

I was nothing without them. Now, I needed to give back. Mike knew just where to push me so I'd get involved and curious. My weakness was worse than his. A pretty face plus a mystery? Hell. He had my number. Recognizing that fact, I backed off Betty Jo. It was for the best. Being related to the Wicked Legion made her off-limits. I knew better than to go there.

However, my fool dick didn't give a shit. Between it being semi-hard from the smell of her hair and the sound of her voice, and my goddamn heart thinking dumbass forever crap, it was time my brain got in gear. But that was easier said than done.

As we walked back, Betty Jo got ahead of me. My gaze drifted to her ass.

She walked with a rock-and-roll strut. The kind that laid down a beat. Her hips swayed from side to side, and the motion of each step plumped up and out on one side as the other rolled down and in. When she turned to see what was keeping me, she caught me looking.

"Like what you see?"

Hell. Yes. "You got a bit of grass on your ass," I lied to cover up my interest.

She did that thing. A cute turn and turn again to try to see what I was looking at. Before you knew it, she'd done a complete three-sixty. "Where?" She brushed her hands over her jeans.

I reached out and flicked off an imaginary blade of grass.

It was tempting to make another swipe. This close, I could feel her taking up space even without looking. It was as if I'd already dialed into everything she was.

Our eyes met, and my hand settled on her hip.

It took everything in me not to drag her close.

"I think I got it."

She licked her bottom lip.

My fingers begged to latch onto her and never let go.

"What the hell is going on?"

A black-haired biker in full Wicked Legion colors strode up. The patch on his vest said "President," and there was the telltale entourage of syco-phants behind him, ready to beat the shit out of me.

I dropped my hand and stepped away from Betty Jo, drawing their attention. "None of your fucking business." As my hand swung away, it automatically touched where my knife sheath should hang at my waist. But we'd gone "incognito" today, and it wasn't there. That didn't mean I was unarmed, only not broadcasting the fact.

"Big talk from a fucking Destroyer."

Betty Jo made a soft noise as she sucked in her breath. I glanced to make certain she wasn't in trouble. But she was smart and had already stepped away, creating further distance between us and, more importantly, away from them.

"Ain't talk."

I had a hunting blade hidden in my boot and a curved karambit sheathed in the leather cuff around my wrist. If shit went down, I had at least two equalizers.

The tent with the parts was within view, and Big Mike and a prospect were already en route to even out the fight. However, I should at least try to be nice. I held up my hands as if to show I wasn't a threat. "Ain't nothing going on."

"Don't give a rat's ass. You were touching my wife." The black-haired President stepped forward, and his buddies flanked either side, crowding in.

"Ex-wife," Betty Jo interjected with a heavy emphasis on "ex."

"Which still makes you off-limits for a no-good Destroyer."

There's a point when a man has a choice. Let the world treat you like a doormat, or be the boot. I led with my left and had my right cocked immediately behind it. The left landed high because her ex ducked, so it clipped him on the eyebrow, but my right undercut caught him at the sweet spot under his chin. It rocked him backward a good two feet. The man directly behind him kept him from going down and then shoved him to the side to get a piece of me.

The two flanking their president were already there. One of them went down when I caught his nose with my elbow. The mother-fucking impact stung like a bee and sent jangles all the way down to my fingertips. I shook it out. That gave the other guy a chance to tackle me.

We rolled around on the ground a bit. He was a good scrapper. It took everything I had to keep from getting pinned and worse.

From the grunts and yells around me, Big Mike had waded in. There wasn't time to see how he was doing because this fucktard was giving me a good run for the money.

But we were outnumbered. I felt a boot graze my skull.

It missed that time. I couldn't count on whoever sent it missing a second time, so I quit fucking around with trying to control the asshole on top of me and instead clamped down around his head.

That meant I could slip out the tiny blade at my wrist.

When he broke free, I swept upwards with it in my fist. I made contact around his ribs but barely caught rather than gutting him. He rolled off me, screaming.

"Motherfucker stabbed me!" He squealed like a stuck pig. I pulled the big knife from my boot and rolled to my feet with both blades ready.

I overshot it and landed on my ass, but quickly got a knee under me and spun around, holding the bigger knife ready for any taker to be stupid enough to wade in.

Big Mike was still standing, and so was the enforcer from Henderson. The prospect was down, either out cold or dead. Two Wicked Legion were on the ground, the guy I caught with my little blade and a scrawny fucker who looked like he'd had his clock cleaned.

The president hung back, eyes wide and dazed. Good. I set off for him, ignoring the closer ones.

At his side was a snake of a man. I could tell he was the kind who would stab you in the back. But I shoved through his defenses, slicing at him with the claw-shaped blade, and then faked a swipe at his boss.

The president stumbled back.

This time there wasn't anyone there to catch him. He went to the dirt. I scrambled on top of him, holding the big hunting blade at his throat. "Call 'em off!" I ordered. I repeated myself for good measure. I could feel that shifty asshole breathing down my neck. There was no telling what I was going to die from, gun or blade, but I knew deep in my soul that he had drawn something.

"Bones," that was all the president croaked. There was a shuffled retreat behind me, and I breathed a little easier.

"We had a truce!" One of the Wicked Legion on the sidelines complained like a little bitch.

"Oh, yeah?" Big Mike's voice was louder than that whiny twit. "Then why the fuck are you stealing parts from us?"

"What the fuck is he talking about?" That was the refrain all around. Except I could see in the president's eyes, he knew.

"We tracked them right to you. Want to explain?" I shifted my grip on the knife slightly so I wouldn't cut his throat out if he wiggled wrong. Rarely did I get this close with any blade despite how often I practiced with them. But this one was new. I'd forged the damn thing. I was razor sharp, and I could hear the alloy's thirst. It wanted to kill. When I made it, I gave it that intent. But until this moment, hadn't realized what I'd unleashed.

"Fuck off."

"I wouldn't say that with Fin's knife at your throat if I was you." Big Mike stepped in. He had a gun held on Bones. Thank God he had my back like that. I don't think I would have still been breathing without it.

To prove Mike wasn't lying, I let the edge press into his skin. When he inhaled, my blade got its first taste of blood. The echoes of the hammer on metal sang in my mind. Imaginary, yes, but an artisan knows their creation's personality from the first hammer blow.

He flinched from the sting. His breathing shifted to shorter, more cautious breaths.

"We didn't steal your parts," he said carefully.

I spit on the ground near his head. "Doesn't mean shit. You have them."

"Technically, we don't." Bones, the one with the gun, pointed at Betty Jo's dad. "He does."

Fuck.

Even the whiner went quiet. In that quiet, Betty Jo piped up. "And where did he get 'em from?"

That was the million-dollar question. One we didn't need an answer for, Betty Jo's sarcasm told us the truth.

Her dad stepped away from the tent and spoke to the man underneath me. "I ain't going down for your shit, Roger. What the fuck were you thinking, stealing from Destroyers? That's fucking stupid."

He turned to Big Mike and put a hand on his own chest. "I swear I didn't know. I swear it."

"He's lying." Roger, the president, pushed at my wrist holding the blade.

"I don't think he is," I replied and kept the pressure on. Only a fool would keep up this fight. I had gravity on my side. Old Roger didn't want to die, so he kept fighting. As long as he did, I wasn't going to make it easier.

"Neither do I," Big Mike dragged out another gun and aimed it in my direction.

I knew he was an excellent shot. But no man can aim at two targets at once. I hoped like hell he was paying more attention to Bones than Roger. Because if he wasn't, I might have to cut Roger's throat in front of a growing crowd of witnesses. "Don't move a fucking muscle," I whispered to Roger. "I might slip."

The tip of the little blade in my left hand was against his ball sack. I smiled at my victim because no matter what he did, he was going to get cut. How badly was completely up to him.

The muscles in Roger's throat worked as he tried to swallow. The strain he was putting on my wrist showed in the red veins that stood out on his forehead.

Then we all heard it. Sirens.

"Fuck."

"Party's over!" Big Mike yelled.

I rolled off Roger and grabbed our prospect off the ground. We hauled ass to the van and got inside while it was rolling.

Big Mike fell into me as we rounded a corner. He was laughing like a lunatic. "God dammit, that was fun."

The prospect woke up and started giggling along. The enforcer from Henderson shook his head and tried to hide a smile. "Kicked their asses good. Well, some of us." He slapped the kid on the back. "You'll learn how to duck one of these days."

The driver and others joked around as we rolled with the sway of the vehicle. The sirens we'd heard soon were long distant.

We'd gotten away with only a few bruises to show for our trouble. At least two Wicked Legion bore my marks. The stories of what happened shot around the cabin.

"Shit, Fin, you were gonna kill him, weren't you?" The second prospect's eyes bugged out a little as he talked. Obviously, he was too new to have heard any rumors.

Big Mike slapped me on the back. "That's our Fin. The best with a knife, and the best knives. Let me see that boot knife. I think I want one."

I flicked it back out of the hilt and wiped it off. I hadn't had time to do a proper job of it before. "Here. Don't cut yourself."

Big Mike held the blade carefully and admired it. I'd crafted it with clean lines, a utilitarian grip, and a simple drop point, but a custom tri-metal inlay near the guard to give it style. He carefully tapped the edge.

"Razor-fucking sharp." He picked up a scrap of garbage that was on the floor in the back and sliced through it. The cut was clean.

Light glinted against the honed edge. Almost as if it winked at me. I winked back, knowing it had saved my fucking life. Sure, Big Mike and the others played a part, but that knife had been my equalizer. Well, it and my little karambit.

I pulled that one out and cleaned it off carefully. Correction. *Him.* The blade I held was definitely a bloodthirsty bastard. He didn't wink or shine or sing or anything. But he was happy in my hand. Happy to be of service and doing it quietly.

Gracing and extending my hand like the claw shape it resembled. The blade was dull grey, crafted from finely-honed carbon steel. It possessed the advantage of both an inner edge and an outer edge for slicing, cutting, and even gouging. That made him my favorite. The shape fit my hand with a hole where my pinky slipped through so it couldn't be knocked away. My larger blade may draw attention, but this one drew its share of blood and then some.

Once clean, I held it up, giving it one last inspection to insure it was dry and oiled properly.

"That little thing came in handy, too." Big Mike lowered his voice. "I saw where you had it. He almost shit his pants, didn't he?"

"To his credit, he didn't." My voice was even, barely interested in talking about someone I'd almost killed.

"Ha! That's what I love about you, Fin. You're always chivalrous. Speaking of, you get any information out of the daughter?"

A ton. None of it Big Mike needed to know. "She and her dad have lived here their entire lives and run the shop for twenty years. He used to ride with the Wicked Legion, but when his brother died, he quit the club. The club didn't quit him, I'm guessing."

"I'm guessing not, either. Do you think he is gonna pay for letting us know about the parts?"

I tucked the little blade back into my cuff. Then asked Mike my own question back. "If you were the president of the Wicked Legion, what would you do?"

Big Mike frowned and thought about it. Finally, he spoke.

"I'd kill the mother fucker. Club business, ya know?"

So would I. "What about the girl?"

He blinked at me. "Do ya think she's involved?"

I shook my head. "Sounded like they keep her in the dark a lot. But she was married to that asshole president." There was no doubt about it. The vitriol in her tone when she said "ex" echoed in my ears. No love lost there. I didn't tell Mike that, opting instead to keep it to myself. If he didn't figure it out, I certainly wasn't going to help him do it.

His face shifted as he thought. "If it were me, I'd probably not kill her, but that bastard looks like the kind of man who gets mean. And, I don't know if you saw it or not, but your girl? She knows he does."

Shit. He had heard her. I rubbed my beard, trying to talk myself out of volunteering for stupidity. Then his words sunk in. "She ain't my girl."

He laughed his ass off at me for that one. "Your hand was on her ass. So, I call bullshit. Anyone else?"

They all nodded, agreeing with Big Mike.

Fuckers.

CHAPTER 5

Roger glowered at my father and I the whole time the police questioned us.

No, we didn't know anyone in the other group. And, no, we didn't know why they were fighting, only that they were.

What did they look like? *Like bikers.* Even though I could detail every color of Fin's eyes, from blue to green to pale yellow-brown, I wasn't going to give the police anything more than "beards and leather."

One of the biggest rules of any club is that you don't say anything to the police.

My father was even cagier.

Theo hung around, cut magically gone, pretending to be a supportive relative, but I knew he was listening to every word so he could report them back to Roger. It took forever, and we lost out on all of the afternoon's sales.

When the police asked why we thought they'd picked our tent, I answered quickly. "They bought a set of leather saddlebags from me."

That caught their attention, and not in a good way. But it was better they think that the leather was the only reason they'd stopped by and not go snooping around the junk Pa had on display.

If those parts were stolen, like Mike said, we could find ourselves in deeper shit than just a ruckus between rival biker groups. I answered as much as I could yet kept it vague.

Bones shadowed Theo now that the spotlight was on me. His eyes narrowed as I described the leather. I made the mistake of looking at him during a lull in the questions. He rubbed his fingers together like he was feeling a hundred-dollar bill between them. Then he pointed his index finger at me, squinted, and pulled the proverbial trigger.

The police officer talking to me followed my attention. "Everything okay over there?"

Theo, clueless, shrugged and said it was. Bones mimicked Theo's gesture with an added, aw shucks, good ol' boy smile for good measure. If you hadn't seen his mean face, you might think it was real. But there was nothing authentic except for his vileness. Even when I was married to Roger, Bones was a right asshole.

I glanced at the small cluster of Roger and his lackeys. He hadn't stopped staring at me. As if suddenly I was much more interesting than I had been all those years I'd been married to him. My heart threatened to care. I locked that down, remembering all the insults, all the pain, all the sorrow he never gave two shits about. It did little good.

Instead, I rested my hand on my hip. It was slightly farther back than I normally set it because that's where Fin's hand had been.

The action thrust my tits out, and the cop lost his place in the conversation. When he finally looked up at my face, I smiled. Not my normal one, but the acceptable one. Demure, non-threatening, soft without being flirtatious, and one I practiced on the daily for the customers in the shop. It was like everything else in my life. Restrained. I was damn sick of all of it.

Too soon, the police left.

Roger strode up and stood beside me. His hand was on my elbow. He caught my father's eye. "Wrench, pay attention."

I tried to step away. It was an instinctual thing. I knew that tone.

Roger's fingers tightened on my arm painfully. He dug in hard, and it hit the nerves that clustered near the joint. My knees buckled from the pain.

He twisted his grip, and I cried out.

"This is a warning." He yanked on my arm. A sharp, sudden pain shot through my shoulder, and my bicep started twitching, which sent a loop of white-hot agony from elbow to shoulder and back. When he finally let me go, my arm hung like a limp noodle. My fingers were cramped up like a dead spider. I didn't dare breathe any deeper than a pant because the pain came back each time I gulped in.

Slowly, my fingers regained feeling. My shoulder still hurt, and I couldn't move it without the tears pooling in my eyes.

Bones stood in front of me and surveyed the damage. "I want my money back, and you're going to make me a set of saddle bags by next week. Else I'll finish what Roger started, and you'll never use that arm again."

He spat in my face.

I made the mistake of lifting my arm to wipe it away and dropped to the ground, unable to even scream.

There was a time, long ago, that learned the right breathing techniques when in labor. I never got to use them until that moment. I counted as I breathed out, then carefully breathed in, being extremely cautious not to do it quickly. Back out with the counting, blowing the pain away.

After about ten cycles, I was dizzy, and the ache hadn't stopped.

"Get up, Betty Jo."

I glared at my father. *If I could, I would.* I thought at him. The words didn't want to come out. I shook my head.

"People are staring."

Let 'em.

A child giggled and pointed. Okay. I can deal with a lot, but not being the laughing stock of some ill-mannered future felon. I staggered because the choice of using my non-injured arm versus holding my arm steady so I didn't jostle it was a fifty-fifty thing. I needed to bear the pain during the first half of the maneuver, but as soon as I got my feet under me, I braced the arm. That sent a wave of pain that threatened to send me down again.

Honest-to-god stars sparkled at the corners of my eyes. I let their little fires flame out as the world went blurry and dark around the edges.

Pa got under my good side and helped me walk to the tent.

It took hours to pack. Hours more to unpack.

Well past midnight, Pa drove back to the house. The lines between his brows were more pronounced, and he'd been silent for too long.

"Do you…" I trailed off because I rethought what I was going to ask.

Pa blew out a breath. "There's paperwork in a lock box under that loose floorboard in the attic. Don't let anyone, not even Theo, find it."

"You're scaring me."

He frowned. "Like I said, under that loose floorboard. The box should survive a fire. If it doesn't, I got a copy at the bank where I make the payment every month."

I knew what he meant. When he bought the house and shop from the Wicked Legion, Pa took out a loan from the bank. I don't know how he managed to hold on with our meager income and minimum payments as long as he did. With the money he'd paid in over the years, we could have probably bought three houses like ours or maybe a nice house. Not a run-down box that had creaks and leaks everywhere you stood.

"What about the business?"

His jaw got tight. "Club gets it."

My head dropped, and I let out a tiny curse. "Why?"

He pulled into our driveway and shut off the car but made no move to get out. Finally, he looked at me and dropped a bombshell on my nice, naive life.

"I gave it to Roger as a fucking wedding present. It was supposed to go to your firstborn."

I bit my lip.

The tears came anyway. I choked out, "That's never going to happen."

"I know." His skin turned red, mottled from the emotion he bottled up inside. But being Pa, he didn't let it out.

He walked around the truck and helped me as I couldn't even get the door open.

"Best see a doctor about that first thing in the morning."

I promised I would and did. However, I ignored his advice about taking it easy and not going to work.

My shoulder was partially dislocated. The doctor wrapped it and gave me a sling and some pain medicine. I had a prescription for anti-inflammatory and more pain medicine to pick up, but I couldn't drive. The cab dropped me off in front of the garage. I walked in and right back out because I could hear Pa up on the roof.

There was a ladder propped up off to the side, and sure as shit, there he was on the flat roof.

"What in the hell are you doing up there?"

"Fixing that damn hole."

Oh, right.

"Don't break your neck."

"I won't. I got it all patched up. Put your foot on the bottom rung there and hold it steady if you can. I'm coming down."

I did as he asked and got out of the way before he could step on me.

"What did the doc say?"

"Said it needs amputation."

"What's that?" Pa set the ladder back against the wall and stared at me in disbelief.

"I'm fucking with you. It's partially dislocated."

"Well, pop it back in."

"It doesn't work like that. The stuff around it got damaged and is swelling up. Going to be a week or more before the swelling goes down. Until then, I'm supposed to rest."

"Guess that bastard Bones won't be getting his saddle bags then." Pa laughed at his lame attempt at humor. It was drowned out by the rumble of bikes tearing up the road.

"Get inside, Betty Jo. Maybe even lock the doors."

"Pa, I ain't hiding."

"Do it." Rarely, if ever, had I heard my father bark like that. I skedaddled into the garage. Instead of going to the office or the house and locking myself in, I dipped into the crowded storage closet behind the bays. It was the least obvious choice as there was barely room for the tires stacked inside, let alone me, but it had a sturdy door and, best of all, a handle on the inside. I shoved a tire iron through the handle and braced it against the wall.

Then I listened.

The rumble of bikes stopped. I heard Bones and Roger's voices. There were a couple of other voices I couldn't pick out as easily, and my father's. They were outside, so what they were saying wasn't clear, just the tone.

Pa raised his voice. "I ain't no snitch."

Roger's voice wasn't as loud. Whatever he said got my father to calm down. Their voices trailed off. I waited almost an hour. The painkillers I'd taken at the doctor were wearing off. I listened hard to hear anything. But all was quiet.

I slipped out of the storage room and looked around. The garage was locked. I went out through the house, using my spare key to lock things up tight. Pa must have left with them. I glanced at the roof. The ladder was still propped up against the wall where we'd left it. I couldn't manage it with one arm, so I left it in place. I called another cab and went to get the prescription.

The prescription was almost as much as what was left in my bank account. I tried calling Pa to get his credit card number, but there was no answer. That left me no choice but to pay for the prescription and hoof it home. It was fully dark before I made it all the way back. Things looked a lot different at night.

Like police lights, they're blindingly bright. There was a squad parked in front of my house. Theo was outside. He looked around and seemed genuinely relieved when he saw me. "What kind of trouble are you in now?" I joked.

His face fell.

"Ma'am? Are you Betty Jo?"

The cop and his partner weren't detaining my cousin. I hoped like hell they weren't here for me. "I am."

The one who'd spoken dropped his head. "She's your cousin?"

"Yes, sir."

Shit. If Theo set me up, I'd kill him. Just as soon as I got out for whatever he was framing me for.

"Your dad fell off the roof." Theo blurted it out over the cop who was trying to speak to me.

"What?"

"We believe he may have fallen from the roof of your family's business. Your cousin found him."

I held my breath. But couldn't work out what was real and what wasn't.

"Where were you?" Theo whined.

"I was at the pharmacy." I held up the bag in my hand.

"He was up there all alone?"

I swallowed.

"Where is my father?" I asked the police.

"He's dead, Betty Jo!" Theo screamed in my face.

My head shook back and forth. I don't recall willing it so. Maybe it was shock, denial, or disbelief. "He can't be. No." *No way.*

Wait… my thoughts drowned out all the platitudes and explanations.

I looked at the officer speaking to me. His face was a perfect mask of sympathy. His partner looked pained. As if he too shared the grief.

But neither of them knew the truth. "You bastard." If I'd had two working arms, I'd have strangled my cousin right there in front of the cops. "You killed him."

"She's in shock." Theo had a great poker face. One I didn't think he possessed. I'd known him since we were kids. There was no lie there. But there was grief. "He's dead, cousin. I'm sorry."

My knees wobbled. A strong arm wrapped up around my waist and held me in place. "Sorry it took me so long. I was in Fresno when you called. Hey, baby."

Roger was treating me like glass. My puke-ass ex-husband had his nice guy game face on.

He also told the cops he was my ex but still a friend of the family. They left me there with Theo, who was a damn better liar than I ever knew, and a murdering son of a bitch.

Paperwork in a lock box. Under the loose floorboard.

Oh shit. What if Pa wasn't killed? "I need to sit down."

My voice wobbled worse than my legs. But I made it inside without falling on my ass. Roger set the bag of pain medicine on the kitchen table. Reminding me further of his part in all this. And how evil he could be.

"Would you please get me some water?" I hadn't taken the medicine yet, figuring it would be safer to wait until I got home.

But I didn't really need it. My whole body was numb.

He set the water down. I pushed it off to one side and opened the paper bag with fumbling hands. The bottle rattled as I tried to hold it steady enough to read the directions. There was a small voice that prodded at me to say "fuck it" and take the whole damn thing. Either I'd be knocked out until next Tuesday, or maybe I'd die.

Damn it. That was the same bitch I thought I beat after the last miscarriage. I cleared my mind long enough to confirm that it was two for the first dose, then one every twelve hours. My shaking subsided as I extracted two pills and swallowed them with water.

"Are you going to be okay?" Roger's tone was soft.

I glanced down at my arm in its sling. There were bruises under the canvas cover. Ones the doctor asked about. I told him I got those when Roger tried to catch me as I fell. And when that happened, I wrenched my shoulder.

The lie worked like a charm. "I'll be fine in a week or two. No thanks to you."

"No, I mean, without your father."

Fuck. If I didn't know him better, I'd guess he had no part in this at all. Even knowing his as well as I did, his tone made me second-guess everything.

I blew out a meditative breath with the same counting technique. It was working a little better now, not only for pain but for anger. And anger made for one heck of a painkiller. My shoulder stopped throbbing as I tried to figure out Roger's game. Then I remembered that he didn't know I'd seen my father today. Nor did he know I'd been there when he and Bones stopped by. I had to answer him realistically, and believably.

"I honestly don't know." I shook my head. "He can't be dead."

"Do you need me or Bear to stick around tonight?"

It took everything not to respond instantly with an emphatic *no*. "I... maybe Theo. You've got Jennifer now."

Boy, if I could put my name in for the fucking academy award...

"She'll understand."

Dead father or not—that deserved a side-eye. "You haven't changed one fucking bit."

"And you're still a bitch, Betty Jo. Give it a rest, will ya?" Theo popped open one of Pa's beers and sat across the table from me. He picked up the medicine bottle and read the label. Then he snorted. "They didn't even give you the good shit."

"What the fuck are you doing?"

He glanced at the beer in his hand. "Staying."

"Pa's going to be pissed that you're drinking his—"

Oh shit. He really was dead.

My only parent who gave a shit about me was gone. The guy who'd manned up and left an entire biker gang to take care of a scared little girl was dead. The guy who held me in the hospital. My only comfort in this world.

I sank into my chair, and my breath caught as my eyes filled up. I coughed on the snot clogging my throat, and the dam broke loose. I pulled napkin after napkin from the holder, trying to stop the pain from pouring out from me. Eventually, it did.

I took inventory of the situation.

Roger took off, not wanting any part of my snot fest.

Theo, on the other hand, made snide comments as he headed once again to the refrigerator.

"You are an ugly crier, cuz." He belched and opened another beer.

"Fuck you."

CHAPTER 6

I had a business to run, an old man to clean up after, and orders to fill. So what was I doing parked in a nondescript Chevy down the block from Betty Jo's house?

Damned if I knew. I'd been following her asshole cousin around and realized that Betty Jo lived smack dab next door to the shop. It also seemed that Theo had moved in. No sign of her dad, and I could have sworn she said she lived with him.

Bikes came and went. The club hung out at the house and the shop more than they hung out at their own clubhouse. It made me wonder why.

But the answer was obvious. The parts were there. Therefore, they were being guarded. And if I had the correct assumption, that guard extended to Betty Jo.

I relayed the info to Mike. He informed me that it wasn't a problem. The plan was to break into the shop at night and steal them back. How the fuck he thought he was going to do that with half of the local Wicked Legion in Betty Jo's house, I had no clue. Not my circus, not my monkeys. That was all Mike's.

So again, what the fuck was I doing here?

Being a damn fool, that's what.

Theo had left about an hour ago on his bike. With him went almost the entire club.

That left Betty Jo alone in the house and the shop empty except for two prospects.

She came out right after Theo and crew departed, took one look at a little Honda that got parked in by a monster truck, and threw a hand into the air as she cursed a blue streak. The other was in a sling.

I don't remember the sling being there when I talked to her last. I played back the fight, trying to figure out if she might have gotten hurt then. All my memories came up blank. And because of that, I suspected she'd been hurt because of me. Maybe it was my guilty conscience that made me stay put instead of following Theo to the clubhouse.

Betty Jo popped out of her house an hour later. She still wore the sling, but it clashed with the black dress she now wore. That piece of clothing I liked. The dress hugged her curves. But, it wasn't the best choice to climb into the monster truck one-handed.

She tried getting in the normal way first. Then, bending over, and leaving that magnificent ass in the air as she shimmied onto the seat. She got stuck under the steering wheel. The urge to go help her was strong, but common sense kept me locked in place.

Finally, she hiked up her skirt almost to her underwear. This freed her legs so she could put one pretty foot on the running board, the other on the floor of the cab, and using her left hand, pulled herself into the driver's seat.

She sat there, catching her breath and muttering to herself. Then she checked the time and took off.

I timed her departure with a little lag so I'd catch which way she turned once she cleared the block. Following her through town was easy. She drove slowly and ended up parking in front of a Catholic church on the wrong side of downtown. Getting out of the truck was easier for her than getting in, but her wince of pain was visible even from my vantage point, almost a block away.

I stared at the church for a bit, trying to figure out her deal. This didn't strike me as normal.

Using caution, I strolled past the main entrance of the building. Most places of worship have a side door or five. Sometimes you get lucky and find one unlocked. Sometimes you gotta help that lock get that way. Being downtown Stockton, I'll let you guess which way worked. I found my way through the building to the sanctuary. Betty Jo was talking to the priest. Both were in the front, near the altar. My position was off to the side, so I could hear some of the conversation.

"And it will be a closed casket," Betty Jo reminded the priest. Her voice was rough, and she barely got the words out.

"I remember. I am so sorry for your loss."

Suddenly things made too much sense. I dipped out, not wanting to get caught, and truly not wanting to watch her fight tears any longer. I got in the beat-up Chevy and drove to the nearest Destroyers chapter clubhouse. It was where Big Mike was staying until this shit show finished. I pulled up a stool at the bar and flagged the prospect bartending to get me a whiskey.

"What you find out?" Big Mike didn't waste time.

"Ain't seen her father in three days. I think he's dead."

Big Mike straightened and contemplated what I said. "Huh. Easy way to find out."

"How?" The whiskey went down too quickly. I debated getting another or waiting. The prospect took away the option by pouring another and setting the bottle down next to me. *Did I look that bad?*

Mike snapped his fingers at the prospect. "Get me the number for Wrench's garage."

A few minutes later, Big Mike was on the phone. "I need to talk to Wrench," he said in lieu of greeting.

There was a pause. "Hey, Wrench?" Another pause, then,. "Naw, gotta talk to him." He rolled his eyes as he listened. But you wouldn't know it from the concern he laced his voice with. "You don't say. Damn, I'm sorry to hear that. When's the funeral?" He made a sympathetic noise and closed with, "I'll pass the word along, I'm real sorry, man. My question can wait until you get things figured out. I'll call back in a week, okay? Thanks." Then he hung up. "Yup. Dead."

I counted to ten in my head, waiting to see if Mike would tell me more, or if I'd have to ask. Finally, I couldn't hold it in any longer. "How?"

"Fucker fell off the roof fixing the bullet hole I shot in it."

He had the nerve to grin.

I almost punched him for that. Instead, I calmly sipped my whiskey. "Betty Jo's arm is in a sling. She's not working at the shop because of it."

"Their president let her live, then."

Big Mike pretended to pay attention to the TV mounted above the bar. The volume was down, and you had to read the captions to know what was going on, or not. He had more to say. That pause was too practiced.

I chewed on my beard hairs to kill the time.

"Letting her live might be the worse punishment." He didn't turn his head, opting to tell it to the TV.

I closed my eyes and imagined how the Destroyers would handle it. I didn't like what I came up with. "What can we do?"

"Nothing." He bounced his head back and forth, coming up with more. "Except steal our shit back. That's what we can do." He studied me, then. "Not what you wanted to hear, was it?"

My eyes went shut again, and I shook my head.

He let out a sigh. "I've known you, what… twenty years or something like that?"

I nodded. "Almost." We prospected together.

"Why'd you have to catch feelings, Fin?"

The chair creaked as I leaned back to think about it. "You can't tell me you'd be okay with something like that in our club?"

He stared at me with a scowl on his face. "I beg your pardon?"

"Family, you know, road family, killing each other and hurting their old ladies. Ex or not, I know that it would piss you right the hell off if it was one of our clubs acting out like that."

His eyebrow went up as if to urge me to keep going. When I didn't, he flipped his hand up and back. "I probably would put whoever did it on my watch list."

Mike's watch list was one that no one wanted to be on. Getting your name there was one wrong move from getting your bones six feet under. Or cremated.

"Remember that kiddie diddler you had me torch?" I couldn't help it. I had to poke at him, get him to see reason.

"Fuck you, Fin."

"Just saying."

He let out a fierce groan and put his head in his hands, rubbing it back and forth. "Nationals is going to have my head for this."

"Wouldn't be the first time you said that. Remember Hagerstown?" I laughed, remembering better days. One of our feeder chapters had trouble with a rival club, shot the club president, and was tearing up members' homes to try to intimidate them into giving up their charter. We put their shit to rights.

"Shooting them assholes was the right move."

"Too bad that river was only a few fucking feet deep." I couldn't help it. I started laughing. We'd weighted the corpses and dropped them in, but their heads bobbed right up to the surface. It took hours to swim in and drag them back to shore.

We were so stupid back then.

"Wasn't the first war we started."

"I'd say we ended that one right quick, though."

Mike nodded. "Hard to fight when your crew is worm food." He chuckled. Then he sobered. "That was territory. This is different. What we did there was acceptable, not some quarrel over a woman, and you know it. Wars over women tend to be bad trouble, old friend."

I grimaced. "I know."

We fell silent, watching whatever was on without any of it sinking in. Finally, he spoke. "You get this out of your system. She isn't yours, and you know it."

That I did. "Garage closed up around nine every night for six days straight. Random after-hours drinking meets. But mostly, Theo, the cousin, locks it up and then goes to the clubhouse to get drunk. But lately, he's been returning to Betty Jo's to sleep around three A.M."

I took a sip and continued.

"Prospects come in at eight in the morning, unlock the place, and clean up. It's usually two, but sometimes it's one, and if it's only one, he's always hungover like a bitch. Well, both of them are, but you wouldn't notice it as much with two to deal with. Around noon, Theo shows up and fucks around with his buddies all day until closing time. A few customers came in the first two days, but yesterday none. And today, I followed Betty Jo instead." I frowned at my admission.

"So, you're saying it's a night job or smash and grab daytime before noon? Knock the prospect out and take our shit back."

"For the day job, we could use a half-ton and not tip off the cops. No alarms to fuck with."

Mike nodded, agreeing.

"Eight?"

"Sometimes eight-thirty, depending on the hangover," I confirmed.

"The funeral is tomorrow. The house will be empty. I bet they'll stay closed for that." If it were the Destroyers, they would.

"Do you think there will be a ride?" I asked.

Mike shook his head. "Too soon. When we plan a memorial ride, it's a week, but mostly two weeks later. They keep the corpse on ice until we're ready. Or, cremate him, and we go with an empty casket."

"You are one morbid motherfucker." I poured another whiskey.

He smiled like he was proud of himself. "We'll do it during the funeral."

He was also in-fucking-sane. "Seriously?"

"As a fucking heart attack. They'll all be at the funeral. If not, it will look bad, like they killed him or something. They *have* to show. Plus, she'll be gone."

Hell. He made sense.

"We roll up with the parts truck between nine and ten. Load the shit, lock back up, and get on the road in under an hour. Easy."

I rubbed my eyes. "I'm getting too old for this shit."

"That's why we have prospects."

"What about alarms?"

"Disable them if there are any. Betty Jo happen to let that slip?"

I shook my head.

"Recon time then." He snapped his fingers and called over a little slip of a girl. "Sugar, get your little brother and take that old Toyota out. Let him drive it. Make sure he rides the brakes and gets them good and hot. Here's a buck-fifty to get them looked at." He arranged it all.

They were to stop at the garage, begging for help. With the kid along, and being daylight and shit, they would get inside where the kid would look for cameras and security features. Apparently, her little brother was a class-A wiz kid at everything electronic. The big sister, on the other hand, was a class-A wiz at everything blow-job-related. Between the two of them, they'd get what we needed.

"Did you need me on the grab?" I asked once his plans were relayed.

"Naw, better your face stays out of it. Maybe you should go to a funeral or something?" I'm certain he was joking.

That didn't stop me from considering it. "Wouldn't get it out of my system that way." I set the glass in my hand down. "Best way to quit something is to go cold turkey."

Mike shook his head. "Bet you five dollars you sit outside the church tomorrow."

"Kind of hard to do, since I don't know which church, right? Or when."

"Funerals last about as long as it takes to load up stolen parts."
He winked.

Fucker. And, I did probably know which church. But it was best to leave
Big Mike guessing.

I moved a five-dollar bill out of my wallet into my jeans, just in case.

———————————————————————

Ant was outside when I pulled up the dirt road to our ramshackle
spread. There were two barns. We used one for storage and the other as a
smithy. The farm also had a two-bedroom house built sometime between
WWI and WWII. The white paint on it had been scoured to gray, and the
dust kicked up from the nearby farms tinted that a rusty brown. The barns
were in much better condition since that's where the majority of our time had
been spent until recently.

The cancer kept him from moving around much. Maybe the new pain
medicine was working? I hadn't held out much hope recently.

"Have you seen my knife?" Ant rummaged around on my workbench.

"Which one?" We'd made so many blades over the years that it was
hard to keep track.

"My first one."

Oh. Every blacksmith learns somewhere. I walked over to the mantle
of the door and pointed. "Put that there when you handed over your
hammers."

Ant's eyes went a smidge wider. "I'm honored, but I want to be buried
with it."

I sucked on my lips for a second before answering. "Best leave it up there
until it happens, right?" This was a discussion I wasn't ready for.

He misread my hesitation. "Don't you get on me about my memory loss
again. I got cancer, not senility."

"I know that, but those drugs you keep getting from your dealer make
you whacky."

"That dealer is a licensed oncologist," he countered, getting angry.

I started chuckling.

"Bastard."

"I wish. You got a minute to go over what I'm taking to the fair next month?" Every summer, Ant and I traveled to Renaissance festivals. Blacksmiths were a must-see attraction. They also served a real purpose, shoeing the horses and fixing armor and stuff like that. The hours were long, but you got to camp on-site. When the crowds went home and the sun set, the troupe players and volunteers would gather around and drink themselves stupid. It was like a good biker party, but with swords and lots of "thees" and "thous."

This summer, because of his cancer, we kept it local and short. We committed to only the closest and shortest one. Then he got worse, and I was thinking of canceling altogether.

"Yup. Wish I was going with you." He settled in on a worn wooden stool I kept tucked under my workbench.

The list of shit I was bringing to the reenactment festival was getting too long. I didn't remember Ant's being as long. Maybe I was overthinking it.

"Told you, you could come along. We'd park the RV behind the tents, and you could stay there."

Or maybe, I was taking everything along so I would be too busy to think about being there by myself.

"Staying in an RV ain't the same. Besides, I'm saving her for Sturgis. Not sure how many miles old Betsy has left. Don't want to burn them up before then."

If he made it that far. August was a long time away in cancer months. "Sturgis. Yeah." I agreed without truly saying what was on my mind.

"You're gonna need help moving the anvil." He scanned my list.

"Talked to the festival lead. He says there's a couple of the knights that can help load it in. I'll come home during the week and check on you."

"You should stay there. That way, you won't get behind."

I should. Leaving Ant for that long would cost more than I made. "If I stay on-site, who's going to watch you? That nurse service I got is weekends only."

He picked up one of my scrap blades and tossed it. Despite the weakness from his illness, it still struck square on the beam we both used as a target. The metal hit with a solid "thunk," and I could hear the reverberation of the metal as its quivers of impact subsided.

The damn thing didn't cure flat. I'm surprised it didn't overbalance in flight.

"Add the RV. Tell the nurse to meet me there. That way, you got the weekends free."

"You sure?"

He shrugged. "If it gets too much, it's too much. We should get a prospect to come help."

I scowled.

"What's that face?"

"Bunch of useless motherfuckers."

"All of em?"

"One of the guys we took to the swap meet hit the dirt first punch."

"Jesus. I hope they booted him for it."

I shook my head.

"What the hell? Is Rocky going soft?"

"Dunno. Maybe."

"He better watch his ass, or someone's gonna come up the ranks and take over."

Ant was right. While I was talking to Big Mike today, I looked around, getting a feel for the membership. The crew was changing. There were obvious signs of a regime change soon. Big Mike was probably called in to check on more than the shipment of parts they'd recovered. "So glad we're not caught up in those fucking political games."

That was met with a hearty nod.

"How's Big Mike?"

"Doing good."

"Is he still chasing his brother's wife?"

"Naw. His brother got paroled. They reconciled."

"That is one fucked up bitch."

My snort was short. Big Mike's main reason for hanging around with his brother's family was their kid. He told me once that he felt an obligation to take care of her since her parents were both screwed in the head. The brother was an abusive son of a bitch. And a damn thief. The wife was worse. The kind of woman who thought the world existed to serve them. Vain to the point of ugly. To hear Mike tell it, she even went as far as to blame her own daughter for taking her spotlight. Screwed up.

"Speaking of, you wanna tell me something?" Ant poked me.

"Tell you what?"

"Anything."

"Don't be cute; it doesn't work for you, Ant. You're an ugly motherfucker."

His chest shook with silent laughter. "You've been pissy lately. And missing a lot. I figure it's a woman."

I pinched the spot between my eyes where all my angry thoughts clustered and counted them away. "Ain't no woman."

"Liar. Look me in the eye and say that."

There was no way I could do that. "Ain't no woman I can have, okay?"

"Oh." The singsong of his one word echoed through me.

"Knock it off."

"You dun fell in love again, didn't ya?"

"Told ya, knock it off."

Ant contemplated me with a tongue stuck in one cheek and a smirk on his face. Finally, he decided to fuck with me anyway. "Can't. What she look like?"

I glared at him. Pain meds or not, he'd feel it if I socked him in the eye. Of course, then I'd feel awful. So, I didn't follow through with my thoughts.

"Come on, at least give me that. I bet she's thick. You always went for the thunder-thighed bitches."

"That's enough!" My hands hit the worktable, jostling everything.

"Ain't nothing wrong with liking a soft mattress to poke."

"Cancer ain't gonna kill you. I am."

He laughed out loud that time. "Make sure that knife's in my pocket when you burn me up. Got it?"

I counted to twenty. "Thought you wanted to be buried."

Ant shrugged. "You kill me, you gotta burn me to destroy the evidence. Either way, I get my knife back."

"You'll get that knife back through your heart."

"Come on, Fin, you got it bad. Admit it."

"Fuck." He was so damn frustrating at times. But I loved him better than my own family. Hell, I might love him more than my bike. You find someone who gave a shit about you and took their time to make sure you are on your feet—you took care of them.

"She's got blue eyes."

"Pretty?"

Fucking gorgeous. "Remember those pin-up girls they used to paint on planes?"

Ant smiled, remembering. "Like Betty Whatshername."

Funny. I hadn't made that connection. Frankly, my Betty Jo was prettier. "Her name is Betty Jo."

"Yeah? And? Not a redhead, I hope."

"Naw. In one sentence, Snow White meets a whole lotta Rosie."

"Woof. If I was a younger man, you'd have sold me right there. I gotta meet her."

He wasn't going to. "Can't. She's not mine."

Ant said what I was thinking, and the main reason I was so ornery lately. "That fucking sucks."

It sure did.

CHAPTER 7

You can't start a funeral on time with a load of bikers fucking things up.

I'd been ready since seven. But Theo took my car last night, saying his bike was being watched by the local cops. Then he had the nerve to stay at the clubhouse overnight.

I took a cab to the church. I'd learned a lesson in pain stealing Coyote's monstrosity. Not to mention no one left their keys lying around after that debacle. Whatever. Pa was worth the twenty bucks.

The funeral director was there, and the priest was there. Customers I'd invoiced over the years were there, but no Wicked Legion.

I closed my eyes and stood in the open doorway, listening to the low rumble of voices and the organist I'd paid a fucking mint for. The day was bright and sunny, like most days. The birds were chirping and chattering. But what I didn't hear was the potato-potato roar of motorcycles.

Pa, if he were alive, would have been crushed to know they'd forgotten about him.

My shoulder hurt, but I wasn't going to wear the ugly blue hospital sling today. I opted instead to tuck my thumb under the top edge of a belt I'd added to my black dress, black tights, and black shoes. The helper from the funeral home stood in the alcove, wringing her hands and tapping her watch. I nodded at her to shut the doors.

No sooner than I did, the thunder outside started to grow. I stepped out to listen.

There was something about seeing a funeral procession of bikes that whispered to my heart. My eyes watered as I stood outside the church, waiting for the Wicked Legion to park in front of the steps.

Roger led the pack, as usual.

Today, Theo was at his side. An honor. Behind him, the members spread out. A good thirteen, including the two prospects in the chaser van, pulled up. The prospects double-parked in the lot, closing off the entrance. Then one took point by the bikes, hand on a holstered firearm, as if daring someone to start shit.

The other stood by the van.

My father's honor guard, in dirty denim and leather. I stood prouder. I dipped my head at Roger when he walked past.

Theo patted me on the good arm, his subtle way of letting me know he recognized my place today.

One by one, the Wicked Legion tromped up the aisle and walked past the casket. Roger stood at Pa's head, marking with a nod to each man who laid a hand on the wood. I followed them and took my place beside Theo in the front row.

Roger sat beside me, sandwiching me between them.

They smelled like cigarettes and stale beer. Theo also smelled like fresh whiskey.

I tried not to frown.

If I had to bury another family member this month, I would probably lose my shit.

The funeral went off without any other hitch until it was time to get the guests to the cemetery.

Roger stood beside me, taking lead, not letting me chat with the people who came to pay their respects. At first, I didn't notice it. But as the people milled past, it became increasingly obvious he was putting himself front and center and pushing me out.

At my own father's funeral.

With the van blocking the driveway, no one could leave, either.

Bones passed out the funeral flags for people to put on their car antenna. I walked down to thank him. Next to him, the prospect on the van got a call.

"No shit?" He got more excited as the person who called him nattered on. "Fuck!"

He tapped Bones on the arm. Then more urgently, tugged on it.

"Show some respect, prospect."

"Someone hit the garage."

I froze. Bones froze. The prospect had turned slightly green as he held the phone out.

Bones took it and listened. He asked a couple of questions, including, "did you get a plate?" and "how many?"

Then he turned to the speck. "Get in the van and go in hot. We'll catch up." He jogged over to Roger and pulled him aside. As he whispered in his ear, my ex glared at me. His dark brown eyes turned black in anger. I swallowed, knowing that look. I'd lived under his thumb too many years not to know the cold eyes of a killer staring at me. Someone was going to die today. I didn't know who, but I could guarantee that Roger was angry enough to do it and never feel guilty about it.

"Ride out!" He circled his hand in the air to signal the riders. Every member and prospect followed his command, even Theo. They departed with a roar.

The priest moved to stand beside me. "Do we wait for them to come back?"

I shook my head. "Naw, let's get Pa into the ground."

Some send-off, no?

About three in the afternoon, I was home, nursing my broken heart by picking at an assortment of casseroles. Some well-wishers dropped more than five different varieties off, along with various other food I didn't have the will to sort and put away. It sat out, going to waste as a reminder of exactly why I hated funerals. There was something about them that was sadder than grief. Maybe it was the futility of it all. Food uneaten. Bills unpaid. Decisions to make over a life that had no more time left. I sat the fork down and sighed.

Maybe I should leave California? There wasn't anything left for me here.

While I prepared the funeral plans, I found Pa's box of papers. The garage business was deeded to Theo. He'd run it into the ground in a month.

The house and land were owned by a corporation. I thought he'd been paying a mortgage on it for all these years, not rent. There was more in the box that I didn't have the headspace to address, so I tucked it away, hiding it back under the floorboard until I could deal.

My idle fork rattled to the floor. The thunder of bikes caused my knee to jump.

The front door slammed open, and Roger led the way. "There you fucking are. Get your shit."

"What?"

"Did I fucking stutter? Get your purse and shit. You're coming with me."

I motioned to the food sitting out. "But we gotta take care of—"

He grabbed my face, pinching hard with his heavy grip. "A bunch of fucking food you want to stuff your face with is the last of your god-damned worries. Get your fucking purse, or I'll have a prospect get it. Now!"

My hands shook. "What is going on?"

"Shut up, bitch." Bones walked past me and snatched my bag off the kitchen counter.

He strode out and handed it off to a prospect.

Roger grabbed my bad arm and dragged me out to his bike. I yelped in protest and shut up quickly as he raised his arm to backhand me. The blow landed behind my ear and tore across my face. The rings he wore scratched my cheek. Blood trickled down with a sick, itchy feeling.

I didn't dare wipe it away.

He watched me like a wolf watches prey. That unnatural stillness creeped me out.

With more fear than grace, I got to my feet and kept my eyes lowered. We were beside his bike. The last time I'd rode on it was when we were still married. There'd been a charity run for the local hospital. The same one I'd nearly died in, twice.

I glanced down at my outfit. The skirt was too tight. My stockings were now torn at both skinned knees. The runs stretched up the thighs, completely ruining the pair.

"On second thought, Bones!"

His VP replied with a grunt.

"She's your backpack now."

Oh fuck.

The ramifications of Roger's words sunk in. I was being passed off. Unworthy of riding behind my ex-husband.

If Bones wanted to, he could pass me off to any other member. And that didn't just mean as a riding partner. I hobbled over, waiting silently for my fate. Bones balanced his bike and let me hike up my skirt so I could straddle the bike. My foot slipped off the peg, dress shoes being a rotten choice in riding accessories. But I had no choice.

Roger's eyes still held murder. And it was looking like it might be mine. I didn't dare talk back or give any indication of a fight. I knew he'd make my life hell. What was left of it, anyway.

I held the bar behind me instead of wrapping my arms around Bones. There was no way, even with an invitation, that I'd do something so unthinkably distasteful. It was bad enough I wasn't riding with Roger. But to touch someone else? That would invite any excuse to violate me.

The bike lurched forward, and I bit my tiny scream of pain. The grip in my weak arm let free, causing me to shift my balance and fouling Bones' seat.

"Sit your ass still."

"Sorry."

"You're going to be," he warned.

I couldn't help it. "Why?" It slipped out before I could think.

"Garage got broken into. Roger is blaming you."

"During the fucking funeral?" I yelled over the wind whipping past us. I glanced back at the road slipping away under his wheels. I hadn't noticed a damn thing when I got home.

"Yup."

That was a mighty impressive feat, orchestrating a break-in from the front fucking pew of a church. My sarcastic comment to that point was lost on Bones.

Then it sunk in.

It didn't matter if I was guilty or not. Roger needed a whipping post for his wounded pride, and he'd picked me as the target. It would be smart to suck up to Bones in order to soften my ex-husband's anger.

But I didn't have it in me. Bones wasn't someone who was easily fooled, even if I wanted to travel that ugly path. It was much better to be honest, take my punishment, and keep as low of a profile as I possibly could. And watch for a chance to get out.

I should have contemplated leaving California earlier than today. Then again, if I had, it wouldn't have stopped whoever stole from the Wicked Legion. And, it would have made me look more guilty. Maybe I'd survive today. But there was no way to survive if I ran. I was better off dead than doing that.

The gate around the club slammed shut as Bones navigated the bumpy gravel of their parking lot. I hung on with one arm and braced as best I could with the other, so I wouldn't spill off the seat and land under his back wheel. That would only give him ideas.

Once we stopped, I somehow managed to get off without falling on my ass.

I flashed a lot of my underwear and torn pantyhose as I did. But it couldn't be helped. I tugged the dress down, one-handed, and tucked my thumb in the belt so I could stop the screaming torture that snaked from elbow to neck.

"Come on."

Bones caught my good arm and dragged me into their common room.

Like most clubhouses, the place had a big room with a bar. That's where the majority of club shenanigans went down. Behind it, there was a stinky single-stall bathroom with two urinals. Men and women were forced to use it.

The hallway to their meeting room had two doors. One led to the "church" room, the other to a second hallway and a staircase into the basement.

I was manhandled down those stairs. My breathing picked up pace as I took in the cement floor and the overlarge drain set dead center.

The place smelled like old bleach and something rotten. There was a single metal chair in the center and an almost-comical light bulb hanging from a cord. The stage was set, so to speak. I refused to let it scare me.

Interrogation was much better than other things.

"Sit your ass down." Bones pointed at the chair.

Others filed in. The prospects, Theo, but Roger didn't. I breathed a small amount of tension out as I tried to figure out the game.

This wasn't something the club had dreamt up. It showed in shuffled feet, and the dreadful silence. No questions, no order, no organization was found in this mess. It was because Roger wasn't thinking ahead.

Bones pulled out a crate and set it down in front of my chair. He parked his ass on it and stared at me. His eyes held a note of "now what?" in them.

If my shoulder didn't hurt so much, I'd have shrugged. Then again, maybe he was trying to judge me guilty so he could add his verdict to Roger's. It served me no good to piss him off as he deliberated.

Roger stomped down the stairs, announcing his presence.

"Why the fuck did you bring her down here? I said, put her in a room upstairs."

"Upstairs is for bitches and members. The basement is for traitors." Bones didn't look at Roger, but continued to stare at me as he growled out his reply.

Roger's gait stuttered. If I hadn't been paying attention to him, I might have missed it. But Bones had shocked him, momentarily.

He laughed, a short, evil sort of huff. "Which are you, Betty Jo? Bitch, or traitor?"

That was a trap. "Neither."

"I don't believe you."

I zipped my mouth tight. It didn't matter if he believed me or not. Facts were, Bones had done me a favor. I might die slowly down here. But at least by labeling me a traitor, I'd been saved from a totally different fate. I'd take it.

"Boss?" Theo started.

"Shut your fucking trap." Roger glared at him.

"Prez didn't ask for your shit, Bear." Coyote elbowed him.

"She's my fucking cousin."

Roger smiled. Then he circled Theo. "Are you a traitor, too?"

"Hell no."

"Are you a bitch?"

"Fuck you, Roger. I earned my patch, like the rest of these men."

My cousin was an idiot. I loved him for it, though.

"Traitor, or bitch!" Roger screamed it at the room. "Those were the fucking choices. Betty Jo? Which are you?"

There was a certain point in my marriage where death, or anything, would have been a blessing. And that pissed me off being reminded of that.

And maybe, if I was going out, I'd go out fucking scratching, clawing, and fighting, like a bitch.

"Bitch, and you have no idea how much of one I can be." I could barely get the words out because my throat threatened to close up.

His backhand came out of nowhere.

I hit the cold floor, and the knot on the other side of my head throbbed as my cheek burned. I curled up, instinctively. He'd kick me next.

"I say you're a fucking traitor, just like your father."

He hissed it in my ear, but it was loud enough that others heard.

Theo sucked in a breath.

Roger whirled on him. "You didn't know? He fucking sold us out to those goddamned Destroyers."

Bones' kick nailed me in the back, high and under my abused shoulder. My short cry of pain couldn't be stopped.

The sound captured Roger's attention. I clamped down on my lips to keep things inside. "When you went off with that Destroyer scum, what did you tell him?"

I thought hard, knowing that if I said, nothing, I'd be lying. If I told Roger everything, he'd get even more angry. No man likes to be usurped. "He asked about my leather. Pa's business, how long we'd been in the valley."

"And the club?"

I shook my head, trying to stall. "I think I told him that Pa used to ride with the club."

His kick hit my shins. That didn't hurt as terribly as Bones' blow. But then he caught me higher, on the thigh, and it struck deep in the tissue, causing my protective curl to come unraveled. His third kick caught me in the stomach.

I threw up. Casserole and bile smeared across the cement and down my dress. I laid in it, feeling it soak into my hair.

"You fat bitch. He was pumping you for information."

There was nothing to do but nod and heave as my stomach tried to right itself.

Roger lifted my dress in the back and pulled down the torn stockings and my underwear. "You are a bitch, Betty Jo. My brand right there says so!" His finger dug into my ass where his property tattoo sat. I whimpered, knowing what he was going to do next.

A deafening "boom" rocked the building. Dust fell down from the rafters.

"What the fuck?"

"Go!" Roger ordered.

The *rat-tat-tat* of automatic weapons was unmistakable. Even left behind in the basement, I could hear all hell breaking loose. I crawled toward the stairs, worried I'd be burned alive or buried if the club took another hit like the first explosion.

Sweat rolled down my spine as I pondered the wooden stairs. Already, I was feeling ten times better than a few moments before, so I crawled up them, slowly.

In the main room, the windows were shuttered, but the glass from them littered the floor.

I crawled behind the heavy wooden bar and tucked into the corner where the cinderblock met the end. There was a waitress pass-through that I could view the room through. Back in the day, I'd bartended here. Getting to know the men of the club while my husband flirted with the whores. Being there kept him from acting on it. In those days, the men liked me.

Sure, it was probably because I had been Roger's wife. But sometimes, you can't fake genuine affection. That's why this hurt more than bruises and strained muscles. I was their proclaimed sister. A treasured woman, an old lady. Now, I was nothing more than a body. Not even woman enough to rape.

Someone got on a bullhorn outside.

"Yo, fucktards. This is a warning. You steal our shit, we take it back. But we ain't taking the insult. You bought yourselves a war, motherfuckers."

"We didn't steal no shit." Roger tucked behind the reinforced section of wall near the window.

"Then why was our shit in your club's garage? And, on that fucking truck two weeks ago? You going senile?"

Bones leaned into Roger. "Mariposa lost a truck, and their prospects turned up dead."

"Motherfuckers." He cursed under his breath.

"Wasn't us!" he yelled out the window.

"Don't give two shits. You wear the same fucking colors, and all you assholes look alike."

Another round of gunfire made Roger and the others hit the floor. Glass rained down on me as stray rounds hit the bottles on the shelf above. I winced as the booze hit my cuts.

"That explains the hit on the garage." Theo crawled over to Roger. I peeked out of the gap and watched Roger's guilt flash over his face.

"If he'd kept his mouth shut, we wouldn't be in this mess. You know that."

My cousin's eyes met mine. "But you're beating Betty Jo over it."

I shook my head. He was going to stick his head out too far and get it taken off.

Another boom rocked the walls.

"Goddammit! They took out the bikes."

"That's fucking it!" Roger reached behind the bar and pulled out the shotgun we kept back there. He barely glanced at me while doing so.

He stuck the barrel through the hole in the shutter and started blasting away. The others joined him. Prospects retrieved rifles and ammo and fed the crew until the roar of bikes retreating disappeared into the distance.

In the aftermath, four bikes, including Roger's, were totaled. The rest had some damage, but mostly cosmetic. The front of the club looked like it had been through a battle, which it had. The upper level was riddled with bullets, every window shattered. The lower level was also but saved by the heavy block and reinforcement built into the walls.

The wooden shutters were in pieces. Some of the bars on the windows bent and loosened to the point of needing to be completely replaced. The explosions took out the gate and the bikes, but other than that, miraculously, not much else.

Using my good arm, I swept up the debris behind the bar and pulled out some undamaged glasses. Each man got a shot of whiskey from me before they returned to their work.

Bones took the bottle from my hand and slammed down about a third of it. Then he handed it back to me. "Keep 'em coming."

I obliged while Roger ranted and made calls.

War.

I'd been saved by a fucking war.

CHAPTER 8

"Man, that was cold as fuck." The Henderson enforcer slapped me on the back.

Big Mike smiled. "You've never had the pleasure to know Fin when he's got his war face on. Motherfucker is the best there is." His beefy hand hit just a tad higher and lingered as he wrapped his fingers around my collar. He pulled me in to whisper in my ear. "I don't think we killed anyone. I had my aim up. If someone was standing right at the windows, they'd be dead, but not if they were on the beds up there."

I shoved him off. "You idiot."

"What?" He held his hands out.

I got in his face. But lowered my voice until it was barely audible between us. "If she was on a bed up there, I'd rather she'd be dead now."

He wrapped both arms around me and pulled my face in against his chest. "Don't think like that. Don't." He hugged me tight. I let my shit weigh down on our bond for a moment, then pushed away.

"No sense in dwelling on it." I blew out an angry stream of air. War wasn't a time to show weakness.

"You're wasted out here, Fin." Big Mike slapped my arm.

"No, I ain't."

He tipped his head as if to form his argument in a way that would convince me. No matter what he said, it wouldn't work. I knew him; I knew his ways. He'd have me riding all over the country chasing my tail, one crisis after another.

"Fucking dynamite. Love that shit. How long you been keeping those sticks, Fin?"

I smirked. "Ant and I picked them up last summer. Thank God they weren't wet." I chuckled. Blowing Roger's bike was my idea. When I lit the fuse, I had a second of debate to hit the door or the line of bikes in front of it.

That fucker's shiny chrome winked at me, and I made the decision. Sure, we lost the ability to storm the club, but that hadn't been the objective in the first place. The object was to declare our intentions. We could have stopped at blowing out the gate and doing a drive-by.

But Mike agreed with me that getting a little more personal with it was a good thing.

"Good to see your throwing aim is still dead on."

"What do you mean? He missed the door." Rocky hadn't stopped bitching since we landed at his clubhouse. His men, on the other hand, loved us. Nothing like a good war to make morale skyrocket.

Mike chuckled. "No, he didn't."

I straddled the bar stool and accepted the tumbler of top-shelf whiskey. "Their president is a fucking waxer." My smile was contagious.

"Blow up a man's club, they get sentimental. But you blow up their bike and—"

"WAR, motherfuckers!" someone yelled. Mike's words were drowned out by the chorus of the crowd. His laughter died. I knew what he was going to say. Blow up the bike, and they know it's personal.

I winked at him and sipped my drink, letting the smokey flavor dance around on my tastebuds. Mike picked up his own glass and toasted me silently.

There's always a way to fight dirty.

Later that evening, I checked on Ant. We'd tucked him in a spare room. There weren't the comforts of home here, and I had to double his pain meds to counter the trip. But he was awake.

"How'd it go?"

"War. Blew up the gate, the bikes."

"Fuck, Fin." There was a note of warning in his voice.

"I know."

"You didn't get the girl."

"Ain't that kind of war, old man. There's no getting the girl at the end of this story." One shoulder crept up as I admitted the truth. Happy ever after was a fucking fairytale that wasn't for me. Hopefully, a stray bullet caught her, and she was dead. If not, I hoped she'd be dead soon. When I saw Roger cold-cock her in front of the house, I almost strode in alone.

I would have died.

Instead, I called Mike. Told him what I'd seen. Followed the bikes to their clubhouse. Witnessed the way they dragged her in.

Mike's the one who mobilized everyone. The Destroyers were still in town with eyes on the funeral and everything in between. In about fifteen minutes, the whole crew met me at the gates.

A lot could happen in fifteen minutes. To keep my brain from dwelling on that, I busied myself with tucking Ant in and making sure he was comfortable. "You rest, okay?"

"Hard to, with those assholes making such a ruckus."

"You're just pissed you can't drink with 'em."

"Son, you know me well."

I poked at him. "Sleep. If you're good, there'll be booze in the morning."

He cracked an eye open. "Promise?"

"Yup. Well, that or more of the good shit." I rattled the bottle of pain-killers in my hand.

"Tease. Get me some weed."

I frowned at him. Not on my watch.

"Had to try," he teased. Then tugged the blanket up to his chin and let himself ride the high.

There wasn't much sleep for me as I sat in the dark by Ant's bedside. I had shit to plan for the trip, orders to drop off before then, and a war on my doorstep.

Yet, what kept me awake was the blood.

She hadn't even tried to wipe it away. What sane person lets a blow like that go?

The answer was obvious. Someone who was used to getting hit, that's who. I scrunched my head between my hands and tried like hell to block it out. But I couldn't.

Blowing up Roger's bike may have been inspired by the moment but given a choice of him or that damn bike, I would have killed him happily. Not because of some pissing match between the Wicked Legion and the Destroyers, but because of that damn blood. No, not just the blood.

I pulled out one of my knives and sharpened it. It didn't need it, but the action gave me something to do during the hours. When that one was finished, I pulled out another. I ran out of blades before I ran out of anger.

Instead, it metastasized into something worse. To put a name to it was impossible. Rage was fleeting and hot. Anger not nearly as destructive. Wrath? Maybe. But it didn't sound calculating enough to match the thoughts that ran through my head.

About daybreak, Mike poked his head in. "Got a second?"

I stood up and stretched my stiff bones. "Yeah. Let's walk."

He fell in beside me, and we strolled out to the dusty wasteland. We paced along the chapter's fence line, watching the sky lighten and listening to the nothingness around us.

"Eyes on things say that she was taken back to her house."

"Who escorted her?"

"Bones. The second in command."

I let out a sigh. "The cagey one?"

"Yup, can't figure out his angle."

"Angle?"

"Don't play stupid with me. I know that tone."

"He's walking the fence, ain't he?"

"If by walking the fence, you mean ratting on his brothers, yeah." His face twisted into disgust.

Big Mike was spot-on, knowing there was something wrong with that one. I'd kept my ears open and heard some whispers about him and Henderson. There was a good reason we knew which truck to take down. And it wasn't because we were that good at observation. But because we were good at exploiting greed.

I brushed away an early insect that buzzed my ear. "Who approached him?"

"Can't tell you that. Bad enough you figured out we got a guy on the inside."

I frowned. "He ain't our guy. He's playing whoever you got on him."

Mike pondered that for a minute. "How do you know?"

I didn't. But I knew his type. "Power," I said.

Big Mike stopped walking and studied me. His forehead wrinkled up.

I stopped as well, not making him work for it. "A man spends that much time building up to an officer spot, he wants it. No one is going to put that to the side unless he wants more. And only a fool looks outside for that shit."

"Well. You're right. I know I wouldn't."

"Neither would I."

"This is why I keep saying you're wasting time out here, Fin. You see the shit clearly. I *need* you, man."

"Ant needs me."

"Ant ain't gonna live forever."

I stepped into Mike's space. "Until then, lay off."

His head went back. "You're going to get rusty."

"That's my problem, ain't it?"

"Rusty'll get you killed."

"There's always something out there going to get you killed. It's a fact of life the way I see it."

"Brother—" he started.

"We don't need to yap on about what-ifs and should-have-beens. There's a war going on, and you got someone with a snake held tight against their skin. You know your best move is to cut that shit loose. Bones is a grade-A snake. One that bites. Best make sure he doesn't bite us."

"We gotta give him what he wants then." Mike smiled, but it was the one he used when he was plotting murder. Dollars to donuts, it was Roger's murder.

"Cut me in on that."

"I might."

"Asshole."

"Or I might let you burn the body."

Now we were talking. I'd gladly oversee that.

"Feds are snooping around the Wicked Legion's clubhouse." Mike mistook my silence for an opening to yap.

"Are they?" The explosions likely got on someone's radar, but I doubted the Wicked Legion went to them voluntarily.

"Yeah, and cops have long memories. They gotta know there's trouble brewing between our groups again."

"There's always trouble between our groups," I pointed out.

Mike frowned. "We gotta pretend this is business as usual."

"What you getting at?"

"Stop following her."

My head went back. Rarely did I get a direct order from anyone. Even Ant knew better than to try and boss me around. That's one of the reasons I lit out with him, so I wouldn't have to take orders.

"Don't be like that. You know I'm right." Mike read me like a book.

"I'll stop."

He smiled, thinking I was done.

"But Ant stays here, and you get someone with a nursing degree, club pays for it, understood?"

"Damn it, Fin."

"The man gave for the club. It's time the club gives back."

"Are you talking for him, or you?" He didn't miss an opportunity to throw my shit back in my face, ever.

"Fuck you," I said. There wasn't much heat behind it. Mike was one of the few brothers I could say I genuinely liked. No matter what he did, there was always that bond there that kept me from leaving altogether. He was family. Good family, not the rotten-to-core kind who'd stab you in the back. I needed him more than he needed me. Maybe when Ant died, I'd take Mike up on his offer, share his burden and likely get my ass shot doing it.

"You know you just gotta ask, Fin."

"Ain't gonna."

That wasn't my way. The minute you go begging for handouts is when you find out all those people who had your back suddenly don't. I never wanted to learn that lesson twice, not about the Destroyers. It was bad enough I'd stuck my neck out this far.

"I'll ask around. See if someone has gash with a brain."

"That'll work. I'll be at the farm through Friday, then the tattoo shop, just in case you wanna put a speck on me."

Mike shook his head. "As much as I love you, it ain't going down that way."

There was a moment I let his words strike a blow to my heart, but I brushed it off. This was more than the loyalty of the club to me. It was my loyalty to the club. It would cost resources and expose the club if they pretended to care what happened to me.

Moreover, I wasn't helpless. "Got it."

His hand rested on my back. "I don't want to ride at your funeral. So…"

Yeah. The unspoken "watch your back" lingered in the morning air. "I don't wanna ride for yours, okay?"

"Ain't gonna happen. I'm going to die in some bitch's bed a hundred years from now."

I snorted. "Try thirty. You ain't that young."

"Neither are you."

We walked until the sun started heating up the dirt, and I figured Ant was awake. I snagged the best whiskey left in the joint and a couple of glasses. Mike joined us as I got Ant his promised drink.

We shot the shit until the booze wore off, and he could take his meds. Then I drove home. The itch of being watched tickled the back of my neck. But things were quiet at the farm. Nothing out of place. I got to work hammering and grinding and finishing up the pieces I needed to finish.

Without having to stop every few hours to check on Ant, I got twice the amount of work done before it got too dark to see. I lay down in my bed and listened to the night.

Before long, my thoughts drifted to Betty Jo. Not the last images I had of her, but of the sunlight on her face and the smell of tacos in the air. My dick hardened, and I stroked it, knowing the fantasy was just that.

Her smile lit up like a light in the darkness. And her skin was softer than the brush of a rose petal. I could kiss her red lips and taste nectar as if the gods themselves had fed me ambrosia. With her on taste on my tongue and the night embracing me in its arms, I jacked off. Funny how trouble doesn't seem so bad when you're drifting between sleep and dreams.

If I were a better man or even had the resources, I'd take her. Set her up somewhere I could protect her and wrap her in my arms every night. Then I wouldn't be alone.

Mike had the right idea, dying in a lover's arms. That would be perfection. That and some land and a forge. Maybe a decent travel trailer I could putter from festival to festival with.

The daylight streamed on me, and I blinked. I must have slept. The plans I'd made while dreaming lingered around me, making me want more.

More than hammering and bills and working for peanuts.

By Friday, I was in a shit mood.

The guy at the gun shop tried to screw me out of money. My four o'clock canceled then rescheduled, and then called to tell me they were running late.

I sat in my tattoo shop thinking life was a big stinking pile of shit. The bell above the door rang as my late appointment arrived. I tossed the list I'd been working on onto my bench and didn't even try to be nice.

"About fucking time you showed up."

"Sorry?"

I turned around, and Betty Jo stood there, holding her arm close. Even bruised and cut up, she was an angel. "Hey. Um, thought you were the asshole who canceled then rebooked, now is late as fuck, and basically jacking me over."

She swallowed, obviously uncomfortable. Her eyes darted around the room, searching for others.

That was the smart thing to do. In fact, it would be smarter to send her away.

"You shouldn't be here."

"I know."

There was a space of silence. I figured she'd get the hint and leave. But she was a tough woman. Hard not to admire that.

"I need a cover-up."

"No."

"What do you mean, no?" Her tone changed from nervous to biting.

"I meant no."

Because obviously, a coverup was just code for "a way to trap the stupid Destroyer into doing something he shouldn't."

"You haven't even seen it."

"Don't need to. I know you're a WL woman."

Her face changed. That shit I said about being an angel? Forget it. The demoness inside her took over. "I swear to God, if anyone ever calls me that again, I'll shoot 'em." She bared her teeth at me as she spoke. The fire in her voice plainly evident.

"You saying you ain't?" Poor girl didn't know I was baiting her.

Her nostrils flared. "I am my own person. No one owns me, and if they try, I'll kill 'em."

"Big words."

"Kill them or die trying. Now give me the damn cover-up."

She was irritating and frustrating and, frankly, refreshing. "It doesn't work that way."

"Yes, it does."

I let my face fall into a dopey scowl. "As much as I'd love to argue with you—"

"The customer is always right."

"Not when they're wrong."

"Are you scared?"

Oh, fuck that.

"Listen, to do a proper cover-up, I gotta see what I have to cover up, make some notes, sketch up the flash for it, and probably, depending on the size and fuckery involved with the piece, book at least two, maybe three appointments. It ain't gonna happen today." I pointed at the sky, which also happened to be outside the door, where she needed to be.

Her perfect eyebrow arched. "Okay."

Then she shocked the shit out of me and turned around and dropped her pants.

And we're talking literally.

I was staring at both of her creamy ass cheeks. The same ones I'd imagined in-between sleep and dreams.

"Think you can fix this shit?"

Her hand brushed across a nasty bit of work. The lines were uneven, and the lettering was crooked. They sloped down at one end and had no redeeming qualities whatsoever. "Who the fuck is King?"

"My ex."

"How many exes you got?"

She turned red and tugged her pants back up, giving me nothing to gape at.

"One. God dammit. Can you do it or not?"

My mind flashed back to those creamy ass cheeks. "Oh, I can." Most certainly, I'd love to do those. Shit. That was my dick talking.

"Eyes up here, Fin." She pointed to her face.

I leaned back in my office chair and clasped my hands across my stomach. The smirk on my face hurt it was so big.

Her eyes dipped to my crotch.

That's right, I got a boner from looking at her ass. "Eyes up here." I lifted a finger to point at my face.

She flipped her hair and stuck her nose in the direction of the wall. She covered it by pretending to inspect the flash artwork stuck there. "Roses. Or maybe skulls. I don't fucking care. Just fix it."

"You don't care what I ink on you?"

"Not one bit."

I had to sit up and let the thoughts in my head run a bit because even after ten blinks, maybe even a dozen, her beautiful rump still flashed in my brain. And as it did, the ideas rolled into place.

"Roses?" I asked, just to check.

"Not my preference."

"No? A rose by any other name…" I didn't know the whole line, so I let it trail off.

"Juliet died."

"Huh. Well, sucks for her."

"You gonna tattoo my ass?"

Among other things…

Whoa. That was leaping a bit far into fantasy land. "Let me see it again."

"You're just saying that to ogle me, aren't you?"

"Me? Naw, I'm a professional."

Shit, the thought made me snort. I tried to cover up the goof by handing her a hopefully harmless smile.

CHAPTER 9

After the week I had, flirting with Fin had its perks. Loosening up and letting the sarcasm flow out was oddly therapeutic. I was so sick of the Wicked Legion and playing nice to my father's killers. But I had to.

Today was the first day I was left alone.

Theo was working in the shop and, knowing it was Friday, had a date with any one of the girls who thought bagging a biker was a great idea. Me? I'd had my fill of bikers.

Except ones who could help me. And foremost was getting that asshole ex-husband of mine's mark off. That was step one. Nope. Step zero in the ditch California plan.

With that mark, I could be tracked down. Years from now, someone somewhere might see it and let the wrong person know. I needed it covered. But also needed a tattooist who wouldn't blab it back to Roger or the club.

For that, I needed Fin. He'd spoken of this place like it was a castle. In truth, it was a tiny little office stuck in a run-down strip mall that held only a firing range, a gun shop, and his place. There wasn't even a sandwich shop or convenience store. Shit, a bait and tackle shop would work well here.

Before getting too sidetracked, I negotiated the terms of this deal. "I got one-fifty, will that be enough?"

He twirled his finger to get me to turn around again. "I didn't get a good enough look at the actual piece. But chalk that up to I wasn't fucking ready for you dropping your panties in front of me."

"You're going to be getting a front-row view soon, don't let it bother you. I'll try not to fart in your face."

He chuckled and mumbled something to the effect of "it wouldn't be the first time a customer did that." Then his fingers slipped along my waistband.

I wasn't ready for that and jumped away.

"Now who's being skittish?"

"I wasn't ready." Who was I kidding? His touch was electrifying. Forbidden, and wow, sent a thrill through me all the way to my bones.

"Get ready and scooch back here so I can look."

I took a deep breath and shuffled closer.

This time I managed to contain the urge to flinch when he touched me. At least he took time to roll my waistband down slowly. A stupid, ill-timed giggle threatened to bubble out because I was so nervous. My hands trembled, and I clenched my fists to keep them steady. He was a professional tattoo artist doing his job. I repeated the mantra to myself as I tried to keep my shit together.

He touched my bare flesh.

The muscle under his finger jumped.

"Easy now. Just looking at the piece."

His breath stirred the air, and my skin prickled. But his fingers were strong and steady as he stretched the skin for a closer inspection.

"They had their power supply turned too damn low."

He went on, tracing the lines. "Dull needle or bent. How long did it take to heal?"

"I couldn't sit for a week." Foolish me thought the pain was worth it, then.

He made a noise that sounded an awful lot like disgust. It was confirmed when he spat out "amateurs" under his breath.

I let out a breath of relief. I'd come to the right place. Despite our start, he was winning me over with his confidence.

"Purple." I don't know where it came from, but the word slipped out. "I want something purple."

"You got it." He rolled the edge down a bit more and tugged at my skin. "Can you hold your pants there? I'm going to take a picture."

"Why?" What if he passed it around? Would he keep it for blackmail?

"Because I need to make a stencil, and I get the image under it for reference. Okay?"

"After you're done with it?"

"It gets destroyed."

"Good." I let out the breath I was holding. With it, some of the tension I had built up between my shoulder blades leaked out. But that doubled up the tension in my neck, so I stiffened my spine and braced myself for whatever life dumped on me.

The chair shifted, and I felt his hands set on my hips. "Listen, you gotta trust me."

It took me too long to formulate an answer.

His fingers tightened, but only enough to give me a shake. "You can trust me."

My head nodded, but I still couldn't talk. If I did, I might lose what little control over my emotions that I had left.

"Now, hold it right there." He led my good arm to the edge where he'd rolled down my pants. "You okay moving the other arm? You were favoring it."

"Aw shit, maybe. I... hurt it a couple weeks ago."

"*You* hurt it?" The skepticism in his tone was evident. I glanced to see his face, but he'd turned to dig out his camera.

When he turned back around, he caught me staring.

"No. Someone wrenched my arm." The truth did *not* set me free.

There was a moment where I swear his eyes went almost as black as Roger's. But it was probably a trick of light because Fin's eyes were light, not dark.

"Good to see you're healing then. I hope whoever did it gets his shit messed up for it."

He positioned me and snapped a picture.

I pondered his words. "Someone blew up his bike." I checked over my shoulder again and didn't miss the smirk on his face. Or the little grunt of happy satisfaction he let sneak out.

"That's a damn shame." His smirk proved his words to be a lie.

"Yup, a damn shame." I giggled because I knew his secret.

"Why don't you sit in the chair for a bit while I sketch out what I'm thinking?"

I could do that.

His pencil dragged across the paper, rarely pausing.

"Why not roses? I mean, aside from the dying shit. I thought all women loved roses," he asked.

"They don't naturally come in purple." Besides, everyone got roses. I wanted something unique. That was part of the reason I came to Fin.

"It's a tattoo. I could make 'em purple."

I thought about it for a minute and shook my head. "Don't get me wrong, but I'm just not seeing it."

"Good. I'm not either."

The sun dipped low, framing the valley outside with long streaks of light. It was less interesting than watching Fin work, but I couldn't allow myself the luxury of watching him, despite the tiny peeks I caught out of the corner of my eye. I was leaving this place. With any luck, I'd land somewhere far enough away from Destroyers and Wicked Legion that I could disappear.

"Here."

He rolled his chair over and handed me a pencil drawing. It was perfectly drawn. "You're really good."

"Some say that." He pointed to the swirling water ripples graced with pale lavender-tipped flowers. A shark sliced through them, leaving madness in its wake. The foam frothed upward as it leapt from the waves. "This part starts right about three inches from the curve of your ass and flows up toward your waist."

"I don't have a waist."

He glanced down. "The hell you don't. Woman, you got curves."

It didn't sound bad the way he said it. In fact, it sounded an awful lot like a compliment. "Thank you, I think."

His hand cupped my chin to get me to lift my head. The touch was gentle, with almost no pressure at all. If it weren't for the roughness of his skin or the warmth inside, it might be air. "I need you to be with me."

I swallowed, wondering if I heard him correctly.

"Not in your head with whatever bullshit you got going on outside that door. This tattoo chair is your happy place, okay?"

Happy place? There was no such thing. But I agreed if that would make him smile. "I like the tattoo, but gotta ask, why a shark? I mean, it wouldn't be my first choice."

There was a glint in his eyes as he tried not to smile and failed. "You said I could tattoo anything on you."

"Yeah." I slowly agreed, still not following where this was leading.

"To cover a property stamp, the rule is, it only can be another property stamp."

"That's a bullshit rule."

His face tightened, but I couldn't read the emotion behind it. "Yeah, it is. But you see, that shark? That's a property stamp."

He leaned back in his chair, mimicking the pose he'd had earlier. Unlike then, I didn't look down. Didn't have to. The smug look on his face dared me to argue with him.

I studied the drawing. "You asshole." I shook my head, trying to deny the joke he had played on me. Sharks have fins. He'd basically drawn up an image declaring me as his.

"Some folks say that about me." His voice was slow and quietly forceful. A shiver sparked between my shoulder blades. To shake it off, I fought back.

"How many women have you tattooed sharks on?"

The humor fell from his face. He cleared his throat twice. But the answer still came out slightly hoarse. "None."

There was honesty in that answer. It rang more sincere than all his flirting. His face turned red as he waited for me to tease him. But I didn't.

I stood up and walked to the mirror. I held the image over my butt, imagining the placement and liking what I saw.

Only a property mark covers another property mark. It was probably a damn lie. I'd lived around bikers long enough to usually be able to sniff them out. Something about him made me accept his words as gospel. Moreover, if I was getting anyone's property stamp on me, why not Fin's? It wasn't like I was going to actually wait around here long enough to make good on the claiming.

A small part of me died, thinking I'd miss out on all things Fin. But it was for the best. I angled a bit more, testing the position.

"Do you need me to make a stencil so you can see it a bit better?"

"I'm good." I handed the drawing back to him. "Go for it."

He looked around at the empty parking lot outside. "Getting dark. When you supposed to be home?"

"Why do you ask?"

He held his hands out. "I figured with a property stamp, someone's gotta be keeping an eye on you. Or at least they should. That's all."

That's the trouble with bikers. They all think too damn much. I was going to be so glad to be shot of all of them. "It's Friday. Theo, my cousin, is going to be balls deep in some club whore. Probably at her place so he can mooch breakfast and have an actual bed. All the upstairs rooms got shot up when their clubhouse got attacked the other day, um wait, you wouldn't know anything about that, would you?"

Wisely, he kept silent. So, I continued.

"Well, because of that little event, they have more important things to do than bother me. That means I'm good."

He studied me. Then shook his head before he elaborated.

"Listen, I know you think that. But shit is going down between our clubs and I don't want you caught in the middle. That means you can't come here. And you certainly can't stay here the three fucking hours it's going to take me to get the outlines of that on you." He sighed.

"Like I said, you'll need two, probably three sessions, especially if you want color in the mix. I'm good, but I ain't a miracle worker. Excellence takes time. That we don't have. Neither of us."

Like I said before, there were no happy places left in this world.

"Somewhere else?"

He shot that suggestion down too quickly.

"Then it has to be here. I'll tell anyone who finds out that I'm taking firearm lessons."

"Would they believe that?"

I thought about it. Theo knew I was downright dangerous with a BB gun, having shot his ass with it when we were ten and twelve, respectively. Roger certainly didn't care enough about me to find out. Anyone else who knew was dead. "I'm rusty… and with a war going on, it might not be a bad idea."

"Jesus, woman, you think you got an answer for everything, don't you?"

"I try."

He pinched the bridge of his nose. "Damn fool."

"I ain't a fool." I'd managed to survive this long. A fool would have died ten times over with the life I led.

"I was talking about myself."

"Oh, well, in that case, carry on." I brushed the image away like a queen dismissing a servant.

He snapped his fingers at me. "Come here."

"I am not a dog."

"You trying to piss me off?"

"Maybe? Is it working?" *Damn, that felt good to let out.*

The way he tried to hide his grin was kind of cute. Once he got his face under control, he tried, doing a bit better. "Please?"

I stepped close enough that I brushed against his knee. A shiver went through me, not a bad kind, either.

He placed his hands on my hips and stared me in the eye. "This is extremely dangerous. When they find out—"

"I'm leaving." I cut him off and then added an explanation. "Pa's dead. They murdered him. I can't prove it, but they all but admitted to it. I don't know why, but Theo is okay with that. I'm not. I need to get away, and before I do, I need any reminder of this place off my body. Short of cutting it off, which I don't want to do, this is my best hope. Please, Fin? Please. I *know* it's dangerous. Believe me, I know."

My body shook, and the breath I tried to suck in stuttered. But I powered through. "That day you or your friends blew up the club—they were about to kill me. You, them, whoever did it, saved me. I wish I could repay you, but I can't. The money I can give you for this is just about every-thing I have. The rest isn't nearly enough to get away and start over. I don't know how I'm going to manage, but I will. I have to because if I stay here, I'm dead."

He waited until I petered out.

"Where you gonna go?"

"I don't know. And at least if I don't know, no one can find me, right?"

"Wrong. You apply for a job, they track you through your social security number. You open a bank account or take money from an account here, they find you. Everyone leaves a trail."

"How can I not leave a trail?" This was shit I needed to learn quickly.

He grimaced. "With what I'm guessing you got, it's impossible. A couple of grand, ten would be good, maybe twenty, then heck yeah, but where you're at, no."

"You could make me disappear."

"If I did that, you'd be dead." His voice held all the warmth of a deep freeze. But that didn't deter me. I had nothing to lose.

"I'm dead anyway."

"I'd rather it not be because of me."

There was a tone of pleading in his voice. I needed to set him straight. "It isn't about you, Fin. It's Roger, my ex. It's about him. Always about him. Even when we were married, it was about him. I was a way to make him look respectable enough for a leadership role. When I couldn't have kids, he milked it for sympathy and rode that shit right into the president's chair. Then turned around and fucked every club whore he could get his hands on.

"When your Destroyers declared war, he smiled. Do you know why?"

Fin shook his head.

"Because he knows that this is a way he can get a reputation. It's always about him. Hurting me? It's because I backtalk. A lot. He hates that because it means he doesn't have control."

"He doesn't have control over this war."

"You think that."

"I know that."

What could I say that wouldn't get me into trouble? *Oh, fuck it.* I was already accused of being a traitor, so why the fuck not go whole hog in? "He knew about the parts."

"Yeah, so?"

"Maybe he was baiting your club?"

Fin snorted.

"What? How can I get you to believe me?"

"Oh, I believe you think that."

"Then what was that snort about?"

He licked his lips and smiled at me. "There wasn't going to be a war."

I blinked, shocked into blankness. Finally, my brain kicked back online. "Of course there was. You have a reputation to maintain, just like Roger. It was going to happen."

"Naw, sweetheart. It wasn't. Not until I took a shine to you and talked a buddy into a rescue mission. We already had our parts back. There was no reason to escalate."

It was a good thing the tattoo chair was right behind me because I planted my ass on it so fast the room spun. Or maybe that was the shock. I don't know which.

"This war's about you."

Oh shit. "Are you nuts?"

"Some people say that about me." There he was, back to that infuriating calmness. I could hardly think I was so angry. But I could poke holes in his theory. I was damn good at poking.

"Okay. Wait a minute, you didn't rescue me."

"No?" He looked me up and down, taking in the visible bruises and my cut cheek. He went as far as to reach out and touch the healing cut with his fingertip. The light pressure made my heart go all wobbly and soft.

God help me.

I hadn't seen it before. Or maybe thought it was only a ruse to get me to talk about the club. But Fin was really interested in me. *Me.* But how could I be certain? "Are you sure you're not just saying that so you can use me? Because frankly? I'm fucking sick of bikers and their bullshit."

CHAPTER 10

I'd be smart to stay far away from Betty Jo. But no one in my life ever accused me of being smart. Clever? Sure. A good judge of bad situations? All the fucking time. But doing a thing because it was the way it should be done?

Ha!

No. It was ingrained in my soul to rebel against someone telling me what to do. Until I found Ant and his blacksmith display, it had been my life's mission to piss people off, from my parents to teachers to anyone who crossed my path. Then I lit out of that life and stuck with Ant. He gave me permission to continue living that way, and suddenly it wasn't as much fun.

He'd said that on purpose, and it pissed me off. But by then, I'd gotten a bit wiser and understood there is a time and place for everything.

Like kissing a beautiful woman.

After hours in a tattoo shop during a biker war, wasn't that time or place. Which meant I needed a distraction. And one somewhere there'd be other people to interrupt me if I felt like doing something downright foolish.

"Are you hungry?"

"Huh?"

"I asked if you were hungry," I repeated myself. The notion had set into my head to feed her.

"I suppose." She blinked at me, shaking off whatever spell had sucked us both under. The pull to grab her and kiss her senseless was magnetic, overwhelming, and still buzzed in the air around us. I cleared my throat and adjusted my seat so I was out of range of her beauty, scent, and warmth.

"Okay. Grab your shit. I know a place up the road that's good. I'm buying you dinner."

"You are?" There was a note of sarcasm in her tone.

"Yes."

Her eyebrow crept up. "I suppose you did sort of ask, but that was a shit-poor way to ask."

Well. It was. But then again, no one ever accused me of being the smoothest Casanova in the room. However, she didn't need to know that.

"Ain't a date. Just two folks getting food."

Her face went flat. "Two folks who shouldn't be seen together, or did you forget?"

I scowled. She was partially right. But the place I had in mind wasn't anywhere one of her friends would go. "We won't be seen." I flicked the "open" sign off and grabbed my keys.

She rolled her eyes and shook her head at me but did follow my truck up the highway and down the turn-off. I pulled into the dusty parking lot of a tourist saloon tucked along the road. It saw its fair share of traffic but wasn't bothered much by the bikers from the valley. The best part was I knew the owner. Her brother owned the gun shop, and I rented the space next door from their father. They were part of my family, in a way.

Her daughter, Tess, manned the front.

"Hey, Tess, can I get a table in the back?"

She glanced at Betty Jo, and a huge smile splashed across her face. "You mean in the *private* room?"

"Knock it off."

"Can't, you're on a date." She scrunched her nose up and giggled like an idiot.

"It ain't a date," I grumbled.

"What he means to say is he's too chicken-shit to actually ask me out, so he lured me here on false promises," Betty Jo laughed as she spoke.

"I said it had good food. You saying I lied?"

"Haven't had the food yet."

Tess's head went back at that. "I'll vouch for the food. It's the best around. Get the steak. And as for you, Ma's in the back. She'll want to check out your not-date."

"Send her out. I got nothing to hide." I held my arms wide and turned in a big circle.

"Except me."

At Betty Jo's grumble, I dropped an arm over her shoulders and led her down a hallway that snaked past the bar and their order station. The private room barely held the three tables inside. That's because most of the space was dominated by an extremely large carved wooden bear standing on its hind legs. It was larger than life-sized, and the top half crouched over so it wouldn't hit the ceiling. When Betty Jo looked up at it, she yelped.

"How'd they get that in here?" Betty Jo eyeballed the narrow door and the tiny room trying to figure it out.

"Everybody has that reaction." Tess handed Betty Jo a paper menu and asked me, "The usual?" She didn't even wait for my nod, knowing what I ordered every time.

"How's Ant?" she asked.

"Still kicking. He's spending a bit of time up in Tahoe," I lied.

"Really? The chemo must be working. That's good." She straightened the bundles of silverware she dropped onto the tiny table in the corner and asked Betty Jo for her drink order. She placed a low tumbler of whiskey on the table when she returned to fuss over the table some more and get Betty Jo's order. I sat back and let the sounds of the kitchen and the smells wash over my senses. It was wrong of me to lead Tess on about how things were going with Ant. Maybe I should set her straight?

"Tess, tell your kin to get out to the farm before too long."

She paused, a question on her face.

"The Tahoe trip is one of his last ones." I held eye contact with her for long enough that she got the hint. Her face morphed from happy to almost tears. I had to look away so I wouldn't feel guilty.

"Oh. I'll let them know," she choked out. "When is he going to be back?"

If this war dragged on, probably never. And here I was, eating with the enemy. I scrambled for a good space of time I could risk bringing him back for one last visit.

"Probably two weeks. I got that fair coming up. There'll be a window where he's home before that. Then I gotta send him back where folks can watch over him while I'm away."

She squeezed my shoulder. "I'm sorry, Fin."

I nodded, not saying anything.

Tess rallied and gave Betty Jo good service while I brooded.

After she left us alone, the silence got thick.

"Who's Ant?"

I debated how to answer. "I guess you could say he's like my father, but that wouldn't be right."

Betty Jo leaned in. The curiosity on her face was plain. "Why's that?"

"Cause he ain't." For some reason, I couldn't look her in the eye. The words felt like a lie. Luckily, she shifted questions.

"He's got cancer, I'm guessing."

I bobbed my head, feeling a bit detached from the conversation. Here I'd been thinking I'd take her out to dinner, show her off a bit, let her get away from her bullshit, and I was dumping my own on her. "Sorry, that's not a great dinner conversation, is it?"

She reached across the table and brushed a finger against mine. "I understand how much it hurts."

Before she could snatch her hand away, I caught it. "I know you do. I'm really sorry about your father."

"You know?"

Was I supposed to lie? I couldn't. "I know. 'Been keeping tabs on you."

Her eyes went wide.

I felt like an asshole. Worse, a stalker asshole. I waited to see if she'd get uncomfortable and throw a fit. She didn't.

"The war," she said under her breath.

"More like the swap meet." It was my turn to mutter.

"Really?"

The longing in her tone made me look up and meet her gaze. "When I bumped into you there, I thought I'd died and went to heaven."

"If I recall correctly, I swore at you."

"You did." I smiled, remembering. Spicy women were the best kind.

"How long have you been with Ant?" She quickly switched the focus from her back to me.

"I moved in with him when I was seventeen. Never got around to leaving. My real dad was a piece of shit. Long story short, I found Ant, and through him, the Destroyers, and I just adopted them, I guess."

"They adopted you."

She wasn't wrong. "Huh. Yep."

"I used to think the Wicked Legion were the same way. Family, you know?"

My radar went up. This was gold. I could hear Big Mike nudging me to dig. Instead, I hesitated.

Betty Jo carried on without any heed to the danger. "After the swap meet, Roger got ugly with me. Hurt me as a warning. Pa must have seen what was coming because he—" She looked away. Her breath was shaky.

Pry. Fuck you, Big Mike. That urge to go against the grain was strong despite everything I owed to the club. I scrambled for the right thing to say.

"Roger hurt you?" Of all the things I could have asked, that wasn't the most important to the Destroyers, but getting confirmation of it was important to me.

She detangled her fingers from mine and rubbed her shoulder. "My shoulder is semi-dislocated thanks to him. But, it's getting better."

I saw red. "Say the word, I'll kill him." My fist balled up, and I imagined breaking him over and over again.

She made a face at me. "Let's not talk about that, okay? How long has Ant had cancer?"

Talk about a cold bucket of water.

My answer took so long that she nudged me by taking my hand again. "Too soon?" The compassion in her eyes undid me. *How could this woman be so...* well, "forgiving" was the word that came to mind. In truth, the Destroyers and, by proxy, me were responsible for her father's death. And here she was, giving me that look. I didn't deserve it. But I'll be damned if I couldn't admit that it moved me.

I shook my head. "We've known for... three years?" I had to think back for a bit because it seemed like forever ago.

"At first, it was all about beating it, you know? We were in it to win it. Sometimes, winning isn't possible, despite how much you fight. About three months ago, we began to work on figuring out what to do with everything when he's gone." There was still a part of me that wanted to deny the inevitable. But I also didn't want to lie to Betty Jo. "Now it's a matter of when."

Her attempt at a smile faltered. "I never got a chance to say goodbye to my father. I guess that's a bit different, isn't it?"

I picked her hand up and wrapped both hands around it before bringing it to my lips to kiss. "It is. And, trust me, your pain has got to hurt worse than mine. If I can do anything, you let me know, got that?" I meant that even if it was an impossible thing to promise.

Her teeth dug into her bottom lip. But she nodded. Then she plastered on a wobbly smile. "I'll hold you to that." Her quick glance away got me thinking she'd lied.

Of course, she had. We had that damn biker war looming over us. Our little discussion was a fantasy of the highest order. No matter how much she didn't deserve her fate, there was nothing I could do to fix it because I was one of the fools who had caused it.

We were interrupted by Tess bringing out the dishes of food. Her mother joined us and coaxed smiles out of Betty Jo as she embarrassed the fuck out of me. This carried on for a good bit. About the point where I began to regret bringing her here, they both wished us a pleasant meal and shut the door behind them, giving us privacy.

Awkward privacy. The very thing I wanted to avoid at the shop.

Betty Jo glanced around the room, landing on the bear. "That's one big-ass bear. Who thought carving that was a good idea?"

I smiled. "I did." There were good memories attached to that damn thing.

"What?"

My smile went wide. "When Ant and I first got here to Cali, I got it in my head to try my hand at chainsaw carving. That bear was one of my better pieces."

"You did that?"

I shrugged but nodded.

"That's amazing. But doesn't answer how you got it in here. That thing must weigh a thousand pounds, probably more."

"Well, now there's a funny story." For that, however, I couldn't claim the credit. My shoulders shook as I held in my laughter.

She pounced on the delay. "Do tell."

I took a deep breath to seize control. "Ant was bragging about me to the owner here and tried to sell it to 'em. The thing is, you're right; the beast weighs a ton. Literally. We weighed it." The memories came rushing back.

"So Ant rents a construction crane and hauls it up here. He was going to plant it outside, near the picnic area."

I pointed in the general direction out the window.

"And?"

Laughter bubbled up. I pantomimed the actions as I spoke. "He's got it up here, off the bed of the truck. The crane has it hanging in the air. And everyone's outside, getting a gander on what's happening and giving all sorts of bad advice. Then, as the crane is swinging it over the roof, the operator fucked up and dropped it."

Her face was priceless.

I pointed up at the roof Ant and I replaced for free. "Went right through and landed on its feet."

"Oh, my God." She had tears in her eyes because she was laughing so hard.

"The owner had to buy it then."

"Oh, Jesus. It wasn't even sold?"

I shook my head.

She covered her mouth with both hands and failed to hide the mirth in her eyes. Finally, she got control over her giggles. Then she floored me with a subject change so abrupt it took my breath away.

"Pa bought me my first leather kit. Sold the belts I made to all the Wicked Legion. Made everybody buy them all until they had at least two or three belts they didn't need. I wised up and began making chaps and saddle bags. Things they could use."

The mixture of bitter and sweet in her words and in her eyes was fascinating. "He was your biggest cheerleader," I observed.

"Like Ant is yours?"

That notion was damn hard to swallow. I clammed up, trying to keep things tied down tight.

"Oh, Fin." She moved her chair around until our legs touched. Her arms wrapped around me, and her hug felt like sunshine.

I pushed away from the table to make more space and pulled her on my lap. Then, I buried my face into her softness. For a moment, maybe longer, I let myself feel everything. From the wonder of her body so close to the moisture that made my eyes squint shut.

Her wet cheek brushed mine as she left a kiss near the trailing edge of my brow.

"Hey." I wiped her eyes, and she returned the favor.

"Fin?"

"Yeah, sweetness?"

"You need to kiss me."

"I do?"

She nodded.

Instead, I reached around her and got the cloth napkin. Then, I wiped her eyes properly and mopped my own face so she wouldn't get slimed. "Okay, that's better." Between the two of us, someone had to be the realist.

She snorted. "Such a romantic."

"You want romance?"

"A girl can dream, right?"

I shook my head, denying her words. As I did, I put both hands on her cheeks to keep her still and not give her any chance to escape. If I was going to do this, I wanted it done right.

She leaned in, drawn in by my grip or simply because she wanted this as much as I did.

I stopped her inches away. This was important. She was right about romance. And I had to man up and tell her the truth, not only about how she made me feel, but what I saw between my hands. How badly I wanted her. What was at stake because it couldn't be denied any longer.

"You're beautiful, Betty Jo. So *damn beautiful*. I'm half in love with you already, and I *know* I shouldn't be." My breath heated the air between our mouths. I licked the pink skin of her bottom lip. Only a taste. And suddenly, we were kissing like we'd been doing it our entire lives.

She came up for air first, panting. Her lips were deeper red, shiny sweet, and parted to let in more air. They were mesmerizingly soft. They made me ache from the inside of my chest all the way down to my balls.

"Half in love?" she whispered. A smirk quirked up and dug a little dimple into her cheek. I put my finger on it.

"Don't tease me."

She swallowed and sobered. "I won't."

I fingered her hair. "You can be a smart ass about just about anything, but don't doubt me. I'm trying to be honest. I don't believe in perfection, but damn, you are really close to my idea of it."

The shape of her mouth dropped into an "oh" of surprise. Then she smiled, and I swear to all that's holy, my life changed.

I lied. *Half in love?* Hell no. I was all the fucking way down that damn road. There was no coming back from this. But I'd also be damned if I gave her that kind of power over me.

"Food's getting cold." I slapped her thigh to get her off me so we could get back to the meal. Sure, my interruption was a cop-out—a way to distance myself from all the heartache building inside. This gorgeous woman was my kind of perfect. We fit like fingers in a glove. Our lives were so alike.

But there was no way in hell this was going to work. Sooner or later, either the Destroyers or the Wicked Legion would drive us apart. If I could hold her at arm's length until that happened, maybe I could spare her the pain I was already accepting.

I'd love her forever. There was no doubt in my mind. We could make something beautiful, living far away from our clubs. But one day, it would all catch up with us.

When it did, I prayed she'd carry on.

Because losing her was going to be the death of me.

CHAPTER 11

"Where have you been?"

Bones' face was hidden in shadow. The light from the street illuminated his knees as he sat in Pa's easy chair. I practically jumped out of my skin because I wasn't expecting him in my house.

"How'd you get in here?"

"I asked a question, woman."

I didn't know him well enough to know whether I should be terrified or not. Scared, hell yes. Terrified of being dismembered and buried across three states? That was still up for grabs.

"And I asked one back. How?" A strong offense was a good defense around these assholes.

"Broke in. Now you answer mine."

Funny, I hadn't noticed anything wrong when I walked in. For a moment, I forgot all about my alibi and flashed on the dinner I'd shared with Fin. And whew! That kiss. My brain was all scrambled from it.

"I was at a gun shop."

He leaned forward, letting the light hit his face. "That's new."

"No, it ain't. 'Been meaning to get a handgun. With Pa gone, it seemed like something I better get doing."

He scratched at something, then pulled out a big-ass, honking revolver from somewhere. "Here." He held it out to me, handle first.

"What are you doing?"

"Take the fucking gun, woman. You're right. You need one."

My hand shook as I stretched it out. "This ain't legal."

"Neither is shooting someone." He pulled it back right before I could take it. "You ain't gonna shoot me, are you?"

"Break into my house again, and hell yes."

God, would I ever learn how to control my damn mouth?

He laughed. I didn't know it was possible to make that man laugh. He'd never done it around me before. "Careful. I might start liking you."

"God help me if that ever happens." *Shut up, you fool!*

There was a grunt, and he got out of the chair. He came into the light and towered over me. While he wasn't bulky, he was just large. "Here."

The gun was heavy and all wrong for my hand. I fumbled the grip and was thankful he didn't notice.

"What gun shop stays open after nine?"

It was almost midnight. The insinuation was clear. I was a liar.

"I ate, too."

"There's food here."

Rotten food. I hadn't cleaned out the leftovers from the funeral yet. The stuff that was salvageable got shoved into the refrigerator and ignored because I didn't want another reminder of that horrible day. "You didn't eat any of it, did you?"

"What?"

"The food. It's from the funeral. Ick."

"You're weird."

Whew. Internally, I was mopping my brow like a cartoon character. Outside, I kept up the bravado.

"Why are you here?"

"Checking up on you." His eyes narrowed.

Obviously.

"Why?"

Something crossed his face. An emotion or a dark thought, I couldn't tell which. Didn't want to know, if you want the truth. I'd been flying high after spending time with Fin. Getting rid of Bones was my goal, but some things couldn't be rushed, especially when trying not to appear guilty as heck after spending the evening with the enemy.

"Roger asked me to."

Well. Screw Roger and his demands.

I handed the gun back to him. "Tell Roger he can go fuck himself. And, he should remember he has a new fucking fiancé."

"You're jealous."

"The fuck I am." I wanted to hit something. That's not jealousy. That's anger.

An evil grin crossed his face. "Admit it, you hate being replaced."

If it would get him gone? I'd agree that Roger was the second-fucking-coming of God. But there were zero guarantees Bones would buy it. "Listen, I'm going to be a real bitch for a minute. You gotta promise me any loyalty you got to my ex-husband stays leashed, understood?"

His eyes narrowed. "Why?"

"What in the Sam Hell do you mean, why? That asshole—" I cut off my words and curled my hands into fists. Bones hadn't promised anything. The very last thing I needed was to have an angry tirade get back to Roger, or worse, get beaten by my ex's second-in-command because of my big bitchy mouth.

I counted to ten, then twenty.

"You done?" he asked.

"No."

I added another five-count.

"Listen, Betty Jo. Truth is, there's a war going on. We... you can't afford to traipse around like it's business as usual."

Boy, oh boy, did he give me a good argument to use against him.

"All the more reason I need a gun."

He indicated the one I'd handed back to him. "Don't see you with one, even though it's offered."

"It's too big for my hands. I'd shoot my toes off with it."

I'd managed to say something that got through his thick skull. He held up the weapon in question and admired it like it was special or something.

While he did that, I put my things to rights. I'd dropped my jacket when he scared the piss out of me and didn't feel safe leaving my purse on the table like I usually did. Not with a scary biker who shouldn't be in my house. Which reminded me...

The back door didn't look broken. Nor did the window panels. "What did you break getting in?"

"Nothing. What do you think, I'm an amateur or something?"

Three. Four. Five. "You picked the lock?"

"Of course."

Okay. I checked the kitchen door. He'd left it unlocked. I locked it. Then, I unlocked it again and opened it. "Leave."

"Where were you, really?"

Damn bikers and *their stupid suspicious natures.*

"Leave."

"You're a bitch, Betty Jo." He moved toward the door.

"Leave." And thank you, God, for small favors. Yes, I certainly was going to embrace that title, especially if it got him *out of my house.*

"I'll get you a baby gun." He stopped nowhere close to outside.

"Leave." My volume increased slightly along with the bubbling anger inside.

"Jesus Christ, I try to fucking do you a favor and get a cunt thrown back in my face for it. No wonder Roger dumped your fat ass."

I pointed at the outside and stomped my foot, too angry to speak.

He stopped right in front of me, crowding me. "There's a war going on, Betty Jo. Don't be stupid."

"Like get a gun and shoot your goddamn dumb ass because you ain't supposed to be in *my* house?" I growled more than spoke the words. My jaw was locked almost shut with the tension I tried to keep inside. Swear to God, if I had a gun at that second, I would have shot him. One biker less in this world would not be a bad thing.

The mess, though...

"You got a Destroyer sniffing around. I saw him following you before the funeral."

Yikes. Fin all but admitted that tonight. I hoped the knowledge didn't show on my face. "And?"

"And, I wonder why?" He scanned me from head to toe, lingering at my tits. I didn't like the scrutiny one bit.

"Get out."

"You need a man to protect you."

On second thought... "I'll take that gun." I held out my hand.

He got as far as reaching the holster before he was onto my intent. "You're going to shoot me, aren't you?"

"Yes. See, if your body is inside my door, I'm fully justified in the deed. Won't matter if I shoot you in the back or the front."

"Woman..." he warned.

"Don't you 'woman' me. I ain't your bitch, I ain't Roger's bitch, not anymore. So, you and *all* the Wicked Legion can leave me the fuck alone."

"Can't."

"Fine. Play it that way." I trotted to the rack where Pa kept the shotgun. I rummaged for the box of shells, hoping they were still good. The last time I remember the gun being fired was when I was ten, maybe eleven. That was right before the BB-gun incident with Theo. After that, my father hung the shotgun up and locked away the ammo. I'd dug it out last week, right after the Destroyers declared war on the Wicked Legion.

"Give me that." Bones wrapped his hand around the loaded double barrel and directed it at the ceiling.

Before he could get it out of my hands, I pulled the trigger.

The blast echoed through the house, making my ears ring and barely missing his face. Bones released his grip and took two steps back.

That was all I needed. I took aim at his ugly ass. He lit out the back door at a good clip.

But he had to start his bike, which gave me a moment to catch up and take aim again.

"Fuck you, Betty Jo!" He tore off before I got the second shot off. So, I missed.

The dog next door started barking.

The neighbors across the street flipped their house lights on. A car alarm blared.

I didn't hit nothing. The birdshot in the gun barely went forty feet. Bad powder. Bones lucked out tonight.

"Everything okay?" The neighbor poked his head out, but not the rest of him.

"Just fine. Scared away a critter." An ornery biker critter.

He went as far as to look up and down the block. "Was it a raccoon? They've been getting in the garbage lately."

"Yup," I lied.

"Okay. Good thing it ain't rats. And don't go shooting my house with that thing, okay?"

"You got it."

I waved at him as he locked up tight. The rest of the neighborhood was dead ignorant and quiet. Even that stupid mutt stopped yapping when he figured out it did no good. Damn. I could have been murdered, and no one would have cared.

"You hit him?"

I yelped. Fin stood in the shadows.

"Jesus! You scared the shit out of me."

"Did you hit him?" he asked again.

I put my hand over my racing heart and tried to calm myself down. He'd taken a dozen years off my life, spooking me like that.

"Unfortunately, no. The shells are too old." I rested the shotgun at my hip. It felt right there.

Fin stared at the street. "That was Bones, right?"

"I shouldn't be talking to you. Not here."
Holy shit, he could have been killed if Bones saw him. "Get inside. Someone is going to see you."

He eyed the open back door with something like regret. "Maybe another night. You okay?"

"Just fine. I got about thirty more shells filled with birdshot to fire off in case I need it."

"Birdshot is no good. I'll bring you some slugs tomorrow."

That would be great, except… "Why are you here?"

"Followed you home."

"You can't do that. Bones is on to you, and probably some of the others are, too."

A smile spread across his face. "Really?"

"Take this seriously, damn it."

That got his chest shaking—he was laughing at me. For a second, I contemplated whether point blank with expired birdshot would hurt him enough or not.

"You're pretty with a shotgun," he said and winked at me.

"I'm pretty all the time." According to his own words, beautiful.

"Damn straight. But really pretty holding a shotgun. Sexy." With that, he licked his lips, then slunk into the shadows of my backyard and disappeared. I walked a little down the path to see if he was still there but saw nothing but weeds and the broken lawnmower Theo promised to fix.

Fin thought I was sexy.

Me.

That happy feeling I'd had before finding Bones in my house was back. I wanted to grab onto it and never let it go. Moreover, I wanted the man who'd given me that happy feeling in my arms. It had been a while since I felt this way.

Scratch that; even when Roger was wooing me, it hadn't felt like this.

Sure, I'd been flattered, flummoxed, dazzled, and, I'll admit, bamboozled. But this was subtly different. Fin never made me feel like an extension of him. Instead, he let me be me. I was powerful as myself, not as a man's woman. That settled into my bones and made my spine a little straighter. It made my chin a little higher.

And it was sexy as hell. I wanted more. My soul yearned for it.

Silly notions. If I wasn't careful, I'd wrap up in that feeling and take a bunch of abuse just to get it fed to me until all that was left was abuse.

Gah. What was I thinking? Was I that much of a bitch that I automatically assumed the worst of everyone?

I had to remember Fin wasn't Roger. I'd seen none of the red flags with Fin that I ignored in the whirlwind of Roger's seduction.

On the other hand, I didn't really know Fin well yet.

Okay, some of the things I knew about Fin were ten times more personal than anything Roger shared with me. And, I was certain there was more under the surface waiting. I wanted to find out everything about Finnigan Curty, the enemy.

Huh. I was infatuated. *Shit.*

Here I was, standing in the dark, making an ass out of myself.

And still, I hesitated, hoping for more. Knowing that I was possibly making all the same mistakes again and letting it happen. That was stupid of me. I debated whether or not my eyes were wide open. Were they feeding rational thoughts into my brain? Running through everything, I had to admit Fin's actions so far hadn't been awful. I'd give him that. I'd let myself accept that as my logical truth.

There was another truth staring me in the face. It was time to get back to my very real life because that's all this was. My future couldn't include him. That would be the death of us both.

"Good night, Fin," I whispered into the dark. There was no reply back, so I had to assume he was gone.

But it didn't feel that way. It felt like he was perched somewhere, watching over me, not in a creepy way, but in a knight-in-shining-armor way.

Bones said I needed a man watching over me. While it was a creepy, sexist thing to say, believing that Fin was out there in the dark made me feel a bit better. Like maybe I wouldn't be murdered in my home by some idiot biker gang who'd killed my father.

I locked up and propped the shotgun up in the corner so I could get a ladder out to inspect the damage I'd done to the ceiling. In all the years here, my father fixed things, never calling the landlord or getting a repair company out to do the work.

Now, he wasn't here to fix this. I fingered the little holes and the black scorched marks that ballooned outward from the blast point and swore.

"Stupid bikers. I gotta spend money I don't have fixing this damn ceiling." I grumbled more as I got out the scrubbing sponges and made more of a mess by smearing the soot around and causing the plaster to get so soggy some of it came off and fell into my hair. I stopped trying when I got soap in my eye. It stung and took forever to rinse out. Then I sat at my kitchen table and started feeling all sorts of sorry for myself.

Why couldn't life be like fairy tales where the prince swoops in and the scullery maid lives happily ever after in a castle? Why did things have to be so damn complicated and messy? I was falling for someone who was the enemy. Not my enemy, but some stupid pissing contest between clubs that stuck me in the middle of their shit.

I should get angry.

Instead, I was sad. My plans to get out of here weren't going the way I'd thought they would. Maybe it was the late hour or the scares I'd had, but I couldn't sleep. I was too wound up to think about going to bed. So, I began to clean up my messes—except for the ceiling.

That would have to wait until tomorrow. I'd figure out some way to get the soot off or paint over it or something. I'd have to go to the hardware store and get patches for the holes. That way, I wouldn't lose money by getting sued for the damage I'd caused.

The shotgun came with me as I got out my notepad and started making lists. Foremost was the hardware store trip.

Looking at the string of "should buys," I crossed out items until I was down to the "have to buys" only. I still hadn't the budget for it. Not if I wanted to eventually leave this shit hole.

I scratched out that as well and crumpled the paper to toss into the garbage. I missed, and it rolled behind the bin.

Did any of it matter?

If I were leaving, why did I care? I tapped the blank pad, thinking. I should go to the bank and close Pa's personal accounts. Maybe he stashed something away? That would help. If there was enough there, I'd hire someone to fix the house, then walk away.

Another thought struck. What if I didn't fix things? What if I just left? What if I truly started over as a blank slate?

With that on my mind, I climbed into the attic and found the box with Pa's paperwork.

Taking my time, I sorted the documents into piles. Ones with memories attached but no real use to me were tossed. Better to hold them in your head than clutter up an exit strategy. If I were found with them, it would be easy to tie me back to this place.

The ones for Theo, about the garage, I put into a shoebox. He could have those. I didn't care anymore. Sure, it made me angry that all of my father's hard work was handed over to him, but I didn't want to run a garage my entire life. That was more my cousin's speed. Who knows? Maybe he'd actually do something with it.

I snorted, not believing my own imagination.

But what I was really interested in, I couldn't find.

There was no rental agreement. No lease to read and find out if I abandoned the house, whether I could get sued or not. Having the Wicked Legion on my ass was one thing, but having a bank on me? A totally different thing.

Finally, my sight was too blurry to focus, and it felt like morning was creeping up on the night. I stretched and tucked all the paperwork regarding the bank accounts and the house into a large envelope. I packed that into my purse. For some paranoid reason, I pulled it back out, tucked it into a pillowcase, and sandwiched it between blankets in the plastic bin under my bed. No clue why.

Probably for the same reason, I set a box of shells on my nightstand and put the shotgun on the bed next to me. I placed a pillow between me and it so I wouldn't roll onto it and accidentally shoot myself, but I didn't want it any farther away.

Fin thought I was prettier with it.

I thought I was safer with it.

Safety was more damn important than pretty, but I'd take both.

CHAPTER 12

"Thought I told you to stop following her." The growl in Big Mike's voice was unmistakable and undeserved.

"She came to me." Before he could light into me like a two-day prospect, I filled him in on everything that happened, believing it was best he knew. Even the embarrassing parts about taking her to dinner. But maybe skipping the bit about trying to suck her tongue down my throat. That no one needed to know.

"Then you went and followed her home. I swear you are like a fucking lost puppy, Fin. Latching on to the first thing that shows you the smallest bit of affection and forgetting all about the rest of us."

"Watch it now," Ant warned.

We were back at the farm, and I'd settled Ant into his easy chair while Big Mike followed us in. That little dinner date I'd had with Betty Jo opened my eyes to a few things. I'd been pushing Ant away and wasting the time we had left. As much as it would hurt when he was gone, I'd regret it if I wasn't there in the end, war or no war. I set Ant's soup on the little table tray and moved it closer so he could get something decent in him.

Then, I addressed the elephant in the room. The real reason my back was prickling like a porcupine on a griddle.

"I ain't your dog, Mike. I ain't no one's dog. Got the nomad patch to prove it." I'd killed for that patch and the autonomy it gave me.

Big Mike's chin stuck out.

Before he said anything, Ant's wheezy voice butted in, taking a shot at Big Mike.

"Face it, all those newbies you've been getting in the ranks are all pieces of shit, ain't they?"

"Ant," I warned. He could stand to hold his tongue a bit.

"He's right."

Well, if that didn't shock the hell out of me. Mike admitting there were cracks in the cement. I grimaced. Wasn't my business, though, just like it wasn't Mike's business to sic someone on my tail.

"I don't think they're ready for this war," Mike continued.

One he'd started by blowing a hole in a garage roof. I kept that inside because if I said anything, he'd toss Betty Jo right back into the mix, and I knew I'd lose on that front. However, he was right. I'd fucked up. It was killing me not to check on her 24/7. That's the main reason I retrieved Ant. To give me a reminder that my actions had consequences. And to remind me that life wasn't all about some woman I'd fallen for.

"Ready or not, shit happens." I shook out the light quilt and put it over Ant's legs, then moved the table closer. "You got this?"

"I can feed myself, idiot," Ant grumbled.

"Fine, but if you spill on that blanket, I'm not washing it."

Ant slurped down a spoonful, then pointed the tip of his spoon at Mike. "You see that? Ornery as a fucking bull. That's because he's in luuurve and not getting laid."

Mike snorted. "There's a cure for that." He held out his cupped hand and stroked the air a few times.

"You both are assholes."

"How is your girl doing?" Ant asked.

"Don't know, don't care."

"Bullshit!" They both yelled at me almost in unison.

"I got shit to do. You finish that soup, Ant. Mike, if you want to talk shit at me, you're going to have to do it while helping me load the trailer." There was too much equipment to pack and double the work for the trip now that I decided to keep Ant close, and I wasn't going to do it all myself if I had a body to help.

"How about I talk shit, and you do it all yourself?"

That didn't deserve a reply. There was work to get to. Mike followed like I knew he would.

"Woman trouble aside, what's gotten up your ass?"

I tossed the steel blanks into their bin. They hit and cried out with sharp, chiming clangs. "That box goes near the front." I pointed at a wooden crate.

"Fin?"

My hammer hit the bench with a thud. "I'm wasting my life."

There was almost suffocating silence. Mike shuffled closer. "Then why'd you bring him back here?"

"Ain't talking about Ant. That ain't a waste. Just everything that comes after."

He leaned against a post. "After, you're coming with me."

I shook my head. "Don't think I am."

His hesitation told me secrets. Ones he hadn't spoken out loud. If there was any doubt, the trouble on his face cleared it up. Something that had never graced his ugly mug hung there. Vulnerability wasn't good for a guy like him. He was the kind of guy who was certain. Even when wrong, you had to fight him tooth and nail to get him to admit it. We'd had those battles. Enough of them to give me insight into his mind.

"I know you want to go back to old times—those days we rode together, but that's not what I want out of life."

My voice strangled on the words.

"You know, I always assumed it would be like that." His tone betrayed the reflection in his heart. "I never asked you what you wanted. So." He slapped his thighs with punctuation. "What do you want?"

"I want a home. A woman. This. But maybe not here. I don't want to be in the middle of a war." I motioned at the forge and the tools around me.

"That's it?"

Yeah. But I had to voice the words. Otherwise, Mike would think I had doubts. "I don't want to hunt people down. As much as there are some folks who deserve it, I don't want that to be the thing that defines me."

Unvoiced were my misgivings about building up the reputation I had. Mike and I cut a swath through the Destroyers' enemies at one point. Tales about those days stuck and followed me around like wraiths. I wanted to create, not destroy.

That word pinched at my soul. Destroyers, destroy… there was no place for gentleness there.

"I'm just feeling sorry for myself," I admitted. "And I'm worried."

"That woman you want?"

"She ain't mine."

He pushed me. "She could be." He went as far as to grab my shoulders and shake me until I looked him square in the eye.

"She could be, Fin. You and I both know it."

"Now who's talking about themselves?"

He shoved me hard. Then held his hands out. "You and I both know that life ain't for me. It never was and never will be."

The boom of his voice echoed off the roof. It left ghosts in its wake. Those ghosts haunted us both. The anger in his voice quieted. "But it could be for you."

"How?" I motioned to the valley that stretched south and west for miles. "There's a war going on. And I'm her enemy."

His reaction was to cross his arms, silently defensive at my bullshit talk.

My hands fell to my sides, useless. "Ain't the life for me either, no matter how much I want it."

Mike studied me, almost defying me to walk my words back. But we were done lying. Both of us had been caught in a trap of our own making. Him, wanting a family so bad he tried to step into his brother's shoes, and me falling for every woman who gave me the time of day. He was right—I was a starved dog running to any affection offered. I hadn't got it at home, so I ran to Ant. Ant introduced me to the Destroyers, and like a damned fool, I'd bought into the brotherhood they preached. I killed for them. In doing that, I killed part of myself.

Lighting off with Ant reintroduced me to something good. Pieces of me that were uniquely mine. Me, as a creator. Me, as a human, not a hunter. Not some beast who enjoyed killing, no matter how good I was at it.

As much as I called Mike a friend and a brother, those pieces were something he couldn't understand. And it drove a wedge between us.

That hurt.

A damned hungry dog. I shook my head, knowing that I couldn't help the way I felt. Maybe it was time I started admitting it to myself and to others. "I call you a friend, Mike. Probably my only one. I hope you know that."

"Where does this fucking box go?"

Shit. There it was. Our way of showing love. Helping a brother out but never saying the goddamned words.

When we were done, he left without a goodbye. Just a "That all of it?" And a nod.

Then dust and the fading sounds of loud pipes.

Ant snored lightly. I cleaned up the half-eaten soup and tucked the blanket around him a bit tighter.

My own words replayed in my head, but they had Betty Jo's voice. "He was your biggest cheerleader." God help me, but she was right.

By any stretch of the imagination, Ant wasn't a good man. He was an outlaw biker through and through. And an awful one at that, just like Big Mike. I'd spent my entire adult life modeling myself after him because, bad or not, he believed in me. That counted for something. I wiped his face where he'd gotten messy and did it with gratitude because, words or not, it was a small way to pay him back for all those years in my corner. No burden was too heavy because it was temporary. Sooner or later, he wouldn't be there for me to carry.

I bit down on my lips, trying like hell to keep from blurting out the shitstorm brewing inside. He needed rest, not my angst.

"Love you, old man," I whispered.

There, I'd said the words. Funny how much lighter I felt for it.

I didn't go into town the next day or the one after that.

Big Mike was right. I shouldn't be following Betty Jo around. It only complicated things.

That didn't stop me from looking up at the door to the tattoo shop every time the bell rang. That part of me that wanted love panted for the sight of her on my doorstep.

Two weeks went by without a word. Not even a phone call to tell me she changed her mind about getting a cover-up on that awful property stamp. I spent more time staring at the parking lot than working.

The Wicked Legion had a piece of shit chaser van that had a string of bullet holes across the passenger side panel where Mike's buddies got a little frisky with it. It drove past the tattoo shop and disappeared from view. There wasn't much in that direction except the gun shop, so I began a mental countdown in my head. As it ticked down, I grabbed my coat and slipped closer to the back door. My bike was out front, but I knew I was a dead man if I tried that route.

Sure as shit, I was about on the "three" or the "two" when the nose of the van came back into view. I dove into the back room and behind a heavy metal desk.

The front blew out with a loud BOOM!

The desk skidded back, pinning me against the cinderblock wall. Instinctively, I tucked into a ball. Tiles from the ceiling rained down and caught fire. The explosion pushed over the thin dividing wall that lay between the front half of the shop and the back room. The top of it, not being anchored to much, fell farther than the bottom and, by doing so, created a nice little gap in front of the back door that taunted me. The roof fell on top of it, crushing everything but sparing me and creating a little avenue of escape that taunted me through the four inches of space left between the desk and wall.

To add insult to injury, the Wicked Legion in the van opened fire on the now wide-open front portion of the shop. Bullets ripped through the broken mess, tearing more destruction in their wake. I pushed on the corner of the desk, but it didn't budge.

Smoke filled the air. I set my back against the wall and pushed with my legs.

Ceiling tile rained on my head for the trouble. But I'd made enough room to wiggle out and dig through the gap.

Alarms went off, and the sprinkler system engaged, spreading water everywhere, but not where the fire was because that part was blown to bits. I choked and spat out filthy water, crawling back under the desk so I wouldn't drown.

Pop! Pop! More gunfire sounded. This time, coming from the shop next door. Probably the damn fool night guard.

The answering hail of bullets all came from the front and then went quiet. A sick feeling hit the pit of my stomach as no more shots rang out.

I listened hard, which wasn't easy over the constant clang of the building alarms. The faint sound of sirens, likely fire and other rescue services, started up but was barely audible with all the commotion. The closest station was minutes away. It might as well be hours away.

The noise spooked the Wicked Legion into retreat.

The shouts as they assembled and tore out weren't distinct— more like organized chaos. Someone kicked the back door. It made me jump. I curled under the desk as the knob rattled and vibrated.

"Locked tight. I think we got him!"

That sounded like Bones.

"Get it open. I need to be sure!"

That was Roger. His voice was unmistakable.

"The whole place is going up." Someone joined Bones at the door because the voice was different. Thank God I hadn't lit out the back door right away. I'd be full of bullet holes by now.

Speaking of… some idiot shot at the lock. The ping of metal on metal made me wince.

More of the roof caved in as they tried and failed to shoot the door open.

The sirens were coming up the highway. Years of hearing them tear by had me envisioning exactly where they slowed to make the turn about a mile away as they slogged up the hill.

"We gotta go!"

Roger swore. Tires squealed. I kept low as I dug through rubble and kept my head down. The alarms still clanged, but the water in the sprinkler system petered out. I flipped the bolt on the door, and it swung outward. Carefully, I waited for someone to open fire, but they must have all left. I crawled out into the dark.

Emboldened by not being shot dead, I crept around the edge of the lot, remaining glued to the shadows of the pine trees.

The front was a mess. A fire truck pulled in, and the emergency lights illuminated the scene. The twenty-odd feet of my shop was a gaping, burning hole. The roof collapsed. That space I'd been trapped in didn't look like space at all.

Hell no, it was as if some angry god smashed his fist down on my tattoo parlor, flattening it and leaving only the little "L" of the back wall and the reinforced wall of the gun shop standing. I fell to my ass.

There was a pit the fire fighters avoided as they waded into the wreckage with their hoses aimed at anything smoldering. It was about a foot deep. The epicenter gouged into the asphalt and left a scorch mark that blasted about ten yards wide from side to side. Centered toward the back of it was a twisted lump of metal. The explosion picked up what was left and embedded it into the destroyed wall of my shop mere feet from where I'd tucked under the desk.

I knew what it was. Or, should I say, what it used to be.

The baby blue back fender of my Heritage soft tail was twisted worse than a pretzel. The rest of my bike was gone. Blasted into oblivion.

They hadn't aimed for the shop.

Oh, no.

Roger made it personal. *Damn.*

Hours later, Mike picked me up from the McDonald's I had holed up at about a half mile away from the scene. The wait gave me time to think and worry. After Mike dropped me off at the farm, I walked every inch of the property in the dark, just to be sure no one was creeping up on Ant and me.

If they tracked me to the tattoo shop, there was no guarantee they hadn't followed me home.

I stayed awake, jumping at every noise. My trigger finger grew stiff due to holding it ready for hours.

About sunrise, Ant needed more medicine for the pain, and I was exhausted.

"They ain't coming here," Ant assured me.

I scrubbed at my beard and reluctantly admitted that he was probably right. "We'll leave early for the festival. I got everything packed." The event didn't start until next weekend. But I knew some vendors arrived as early as mid-week. We'd beat them there by a few days, but that was safer than staying here and getting blown up.

"Not until you get some rest. I ain't dying in no RV crash because you didn't get any shut-eye." He poked at me and motioned for my gun. "I'll keep watch."

"Wake me in two hours."

"I'll wake you around noon, and don't give me no lip about it."

"Are you ordering me?"

"Someone's got to. Figure I'd shove my weight around one last time or two. Are you hearing me on this?"

I sighed. "If I die, I'm taking your ass to hell with me."

Ant snorted. "Son, I'm leading the way for you if that happens. Now please, sleep. Okay?"

As I wound down, my mind circled back on everything. The hole where my bike had been. The miracle that I was even alive. And something that should have disturbed me but didn't. In fact, it felt right.

He called me "Son."

CHAPTER 13

I knew I shouldn't be here, but the usual gauntlet of Bones, Theo, or even Roger wasn't in place when I woke up Saturday morning. Instead, I had the house to myself.

The quiet was blissful for all of five seconds. Then I realized that if I didn't move my ass, the opportunity would slip away. I got up, showered quickly, and got ready.

With a little more care than usual, I put on my make-up and picked out clothes that didn't look like shit on me. Then I snuck to my car and kept a vigilant eye on the street and my surroundings until I was well out of town.

I kept checking my rearview mirror for bikes or one of the Wicked Legion's trucks. By the time I made my way to hill country, I was a nervous wreck.

Then I knew why I'd gotten a reprieve.

I stood by my car, staring at the tattoo parlor. Or should I say, the *hole* where it used to be.

Crime scene tape was everywhere, even at the gun shop. As I stood there in shock, someone pulled in behind me.

"They're closed!" the person yelled out their window.

It was half on my mind to yell something snarky back, but my brain was offline, reeling from what was staring me in the face. "What happened here?"

"Some bikers blew up the tattoo shop and killed the night guard. It's all over the news."

"Killed?" I stared at the rubble and swore there was a bike in the middle of the mess. My heart sank to my toes.

The guy shut off his engine to be heard better. "Yeah. Apparently, there's some sort of gang war going on. The guy that ran the tattoo shop was in a rival club. Cops figured he died, too, but they haven't found the body yet."

There was a point in the middle of that where I checked out. I was on auto pilot as I thanked them and got in my car. Instead of turning left and going back the way I came, I turned right and puttered my way to the restaurant Fin had taken me to. I paused outside, staring at the roof and noticing the mismatched shingles over one section. Tears welled up in my eyes.

"Hey, we open in a couple of hours. Oh, hi, Betty Jo. What brings you here?"

Tess parked her little Subaru in the lot next to my car.

I thought about Ant. Would he know Fin was dead? Who would take care of him?

"Do you know where Ant lives?"

"Sure do. He's got a farm down in the valley. Come on in, and I'll get the address for you."

She unlocked the building and led me in. As she searched for the address, I turned on the TV and flicked through the channels to find the news. But the local show was over, and the events hadn't hit the national news that played incessantly all day and night.

"You okay?"

"I just came from the tattoo shop. Fin's gone."

She smiled. "He doesn't come in until four on Saturdays."

I looked her square in the eye. "The shop is gone."

"What?"

"Blown up, burned out, gone."

She caught a chair to stop herself from falling. "Whoa."

Her disbelief was short-lived as she rallied and called her parents. They assured her that I wasn't lying.

By the time she got off the phone, she was crying. I patted her on the back and did my best to comfort her. It had been my intention to walk into the little dining room and get a last look at that stupid bear, but awkwardness and, I'll admit, a little jealousy stopped me. Tess was taking this a hell of a lot worse than I was. Or, should I say, outwardly taking it worse.

Inside I was dying. Bleeding out from a broken heart. But this little bitch was acting like she'd lost her best friend. I extracted myself as soon as I could, opting not to drink with her. That would be too weird. Moreover, someone needed to check on Ant.

I nominated myself.

Armed with the address and my GPS, I found the little dirt road that stretched between vegetable fields and irrigation ditches. The workers were out in force. They noticed me drive by, but no one stopped me.

I pulled up to a little spread of buildings. The farmhouse needed paint. I walked up to the door and was met there by a large but frail man with a shotgun.

"Who are you?"

"I'm Betty Jo. Are you Ant?"

His fingers fumbled the gun, and I caught the barrel and pointed it so it wouldn't shoot someone's nose off. "Heard about you. You're exactly like he said. Snow White meets..." He looked down and coughed. "Excuse me."

"You heard?" I tried to put as much sympathy into my voice as I could, but still thought I sounded hard and bitchy. That scene with Tess was nibbling on my nerves too much to be any other way.

"About you? Hell yeah. Boy couldn't shut up about you." Ant leaned in and whispered conspiratorially, "I think he whacks off thinking 'bout your tits."

I swallowed. Ant was slipping from past to present tense. A sure sign he was in denial.

"I was at the tattoo shop earlier."

He made a sharp noise somewhere between a "ha" and a grunt. "Fucking Wicked Legion."

There it was. Confirmation that I was to blame.

"I came here to see if there was anything I could do for you. And... offer my condolences?" I didn't mean for it to come out as a question. But it did.

He squinted at me. Then a slow smile came over his face. It creeped me out. I took a step back.

"You can do something for me." His smile got a bit wider, and I could see where he'd had some teeth replaced by metal crowns.

With a deep inhale, I braced myself. Years of dealing with dirty bikers had my guard up. I phrased my reply as a question and not an agreement to something I wasn't about ready to give. "What do you need?"

"Wake that fool up. Maybe kiss him or something. We got to get going soon."

"What?"

He pointed behind him with his thumb. "Fin's sleeping in the back. Bedroom is the one to the left. Wake his ass up. I'm tired of standing watch, and it's noon already." He paused and added, "Go."

I wobbled a bit as I walked around him, trying to figure out if this was a joke or real.

Then I saw Fin's boots on the mat, his coat on the hook.

He was alive.

And Ant had a really good idea.

I crept to the back room and took a moment to watch Fin sleep. His long hair tangled in his beard. There was soot on his face. He had a cut running down one cheekbone.

That made my heart quiver a bit. He'd been right in the middle of that blast and somehow lived.

Very carefully, I brushed the strands away to see him better.

His eyes shot open.

For a half-second he was dazed, then his sharp gaze fixed on me. "Am I dead?"

I shook my head. "No, I think you're alive." My fingers tangled in his hair. He smelled like soggy smoke. But he was alive. That's what really mattered.

He reached out to me and touched my face. "What are you doing here, Betty Jo?"

"I thought you were dead." My voice barely stretched beyond a whisper.

"Thought I was, too. No thanks to Roger and his bunch."

"I'm sorry."

He licked his lips and rolled onto his back with a sigh. "You shouldn't be here." He shook his head as if he could deny my existence.

"I was at the tattoo shop this morning. Then, I went to the restaurant and talked to Tess." That splash of jealousy slammed into me again as I remembered her pretty sobs.

"What is that face?"

"What face?"

He smiled and tilted his head. "You talked to Tess, then what?"

"She gave me this address, and I came here to check on Ant, thinking you were dead and shit."

"And I wasn't." He chuckled.

I pushed his hand away. *Oaf.*

"Hey now, softer, woman. I had a rough night."

His reminder made my heart all squishy again. "Are you okay?"

"Banged up a bit. Drank about five gallons of shitty sprinkler water. Almost got crushed by a wall and a ceiling..." He trailed off, looking up at me with hopeful eyes.

"Everyone thinks you're dead."

"Good." He sat up, and the sheet fell down. He caught it and covered his crotch with the bunched fabric. But I saw enough to know he slept naked. Not to mention the scrawling tattoos that started about mid-stomach and stretched as far as I could see—they were amazing, numerous, and had his style etched all over them.

"You tattooed yourself?" I reached out and ran a finger down one that snaked from shoulder to elbow.

"Gotta learn somewhere."

Remembering Ant's directions, I leaned in.

"What you doing?"

"I'm gonna kiss you. Okay?"

There was a moment where I thought he was going to say no. Then I think he realized exactly what I was offering, and that kickstarted a reaction so dramatic it swept me up in it.

He wrapped his hand behind my head and pulled me in. His mouth opened over mine, and I didn't fight it.

Nope. I *relished* it.

Tess and her soggy tears be damned. Fin was alive and kissing me. And, the best part, I was kissing him back.

Wait, not the best part. He was naked, kissing me, me kissing him back, and hell, not a damn thing could stop us.

Except for Ant not so politely coughing as he stood in the hall just outside Fin's door. "You two going to fuck? If so, I'm taking a damn nap. You two start going at it, and we're never going to get on the road by one-thirty like you wanted to."

Fin swore softly. "Old man, get your shit together. We'll be on the road in a half hour."

Then he held my chin. "Do you still want to leave California?"

If it meant more kisses? *Hell yes.* I nodded.

"I need the words, Betty Jo. Last night, I almost died. If people think I'm dead, that's good. But if you aren't where you're supposed to be when you're supposed to be there, that's going to go bad for you, got it? Especially if they find out you went to my shop this morning. Did anyone see you?"

I nodded, remembering the man in the parking lot and, of course, Tess. "Yes, someone was in the parking lot."

He swore harder. His eyes followed his thoughts. "It wasn't a biker, was it?"

"No, it wasn't," I answered.

"You gotta go home."

"The hell I do."

His hands cupped my face. "Sweetheart, you do. You can't follow me. I'm taking Ant, and we'll be gone. For good, I think."

"I'm coming with you." Such a small string of words. Ones I sealed my fate with.

His eyes softened, but his forehead creased with worry. "Betty Jo—"

"I'm coming with you. Even if you get sick of me in a few days, I'm never going back. I need to get out of California and disappear. Now. Not later, not someday when it's safe. It's never going to be safe enough. I'll never be rich enough or ready enough. It has to be now." Theo had been an absolute shit since I gave him half of my father's papers. So had Roger. And don't get me started on the way Bones was always watching me like he had to memorize my every move in order to report back on my tiniest fart. I was sick of it.

"But you're leaving everything."

"With Pa gone, there's nothing left for me here." I'd figure out a way to close his accounts by phone or let them rot for all I cared. I know it was stupid. All I had was my purse, my car, and the clothes on my back, but nothing else mattered.

Somewhere between the crater in front of Fin's tattoo shop and feeling his fingers tighten in my hair as we kissed, my life changed. Maybe it was comforting Tess. Maybe it was deciding to turn right instead of left. Whenever it was, there was nothing behind me and everything in front of me. I was ready to shake the dust off my feet and get moving.

Until our first fight.

Which happened right about the same time Fin told me I couldn't take my car.

Ant wisely pointed out to Fin he was wrong in demanding I park it behind one of the barns. "They'll find it and know she's with us. Best she takes it with for now and ditches it later."

Not that I wanted to ditch it at all. My car gave me an escape route Fin or Ant couldn't control. That was important to me.

But I could also see their point. The car was a way Roger could hunt me down. Or worse, notify the authorities and let them hunt me down. I weighed the odds of Roger running to the cops over me. They were about fifty-fifty. Something about his recent obsession set my radar alarms off. And with that man, I'd learned to trust the alarms implicitly.

With Ant on my side, I got to keep the car temporarily. But all of the arguments about why it was a bad idea took root and ratcheted up my anxiety. As we wound south, the tension in my spine worsened. I followed behind the RV and trailer, not even knowing the destination but trusting that Fin and Ant wouldn't betray me.

That said, we were going the wrong way. South was deeper into Legion territory. My hands shook from stress as a motorcycle buzzed past us in the far left lane. It was just some average civilian rider, but the sound set my teeth on edge. The car was a liability. The target it painted on my back set my imagination into spirals of doubt and worry.

When we pulled into a recreation area near the Cajun Pass sometime well after sunset, I practically kissed the ground when I fell out of my car.

The place was empty, except for our vehicles. Fin busied himself with hooking the RV up. "Best get inside. Fair warning, Ant's zonked out in the back. The ride was hard on him."

On him? What about me?

Reality was setting in. Today went from bright, to shit, to happy, and then to worry.

I planted my fists on my hips and opened my mouth to let Fin have it.

"You okay?" He paused in the middle of cranking something at the side of the RV.

"No."

My tone must have warned him because he took a moment before he spoke. "I know you want to keep the car, but I have to admit, I worried like heck you were going to get pulled over."

That shot my anger down like a pin into a balloon. "I was, too. And yeah." It sucked to admit defeat.

"We'll figure it out tomorrow. I got a tarp in the trailer. Can you help me cover your car?"

"I can do that. Should I check on Ant first?"

Fin shook his head. "He's okay, mostly stiff from being cramped up all day. I thought he'd be more comfortable on the big mattress. That leaves the fold-out for us."

We were going to share a bed?

Oh wow. My mind flashed back to the wild kiss we shared this morning.

As I came to grips with the notion, he unlocked the trailer and fished out a tarp.

We covered my car, and he tied the ends down so the tarp wouldn't blow off. Then it became increasingly awkward as we crammed inside the motorhome.

It might have been beautiful once, but hard use weathered it. Not to mention that you couldn't turn around inside without brushing up against something.

Oh, who was I kidding? It was mostly Fin I was brushing up against. He almost made it a point to get in my way any chance he could. If I didn't know better, I'd have thought he was doing it on purpose so he could touch my arms or my hips and move me out of his way. But honestly? I felt like a third wheel.

And did we forget I'd left with only the clothes I had on?

That thought hit me full force as I sat inside the tiny little bathroom and second-guessed all my life choices.

Fin tapped on the door. "You about done in there?"

I blew out a deep sigh. "I think so." Except I wasn't. I had no clue how anything worked. There was no convenient little flush handle. I managed to figure out the mini sink worked with a foot pump to squirt water out but was consumed with panic about the literal other shit.

"Food's done." He spoke through the closed door.

"Bite the bullet, Betty Jo."

"What's that?"

"I was talking to myself. Not you."

"Ant does that shit, too."

I heard the clink of pots and pans. "How do you flush?" Luckily, the walls were paper thin, so I didn't have to yell.

"Foot lever."

What? Oh. Now I felt like an idiot. In for a penny, in for a pound. "Where do you shower? Is that in the back?"

"The handles are to your right."

Ho-leee-shit. No wonder the TP was covered. "Mental note, get rich and buy something bigger. 'Cause this sucks."

On principle, I washed my hands again.

Fin brushed past me again between the bathroom and the table. This time, I felt his hard-on. "Are you doing that on purpose?"

"Doing what?"

I gaped. Maybe it was all in my head. I sat down at the tiny table. Fin brushed past me again, this time putting his hand on the seat back right by my shoulder as he walked past. The back of one finger skimmed my arm and was gone almost instantly. I followed the entire thing and let him know I was onto his game with a raised eyebrow.

There it was, the barest twitch at the corner of his mouth, acknowledging he was amused but denying me verbal confirmation.

"No bear."

"What?"

"There's no bear looming over us while we eat this time."

His smile bloomed into a full-fledged grin. "I'm gonna miss that damn thing."

I reached across the table to catch his hand. "So am I, but you can always make another, right?"

He wrapped his fingers around mine and pulled them up to his lips. "Sure can."

There I was, in the middle of Wicked Legion territory, making plans for the future with a Destroyer.

The future.

Eating away at the dark corners of my thoughts was a sneaky whisper of warning not to get too attached to this new life. Things were bound to change. Something told me it wasn't going to be for the better. That thought made me break out in goose bumps.

CHAPTER 14

"This is where we're going to sleep?"

Betty Jo eyed the fold-out bench with concern. I tugged down my sleeping bag and laid it out over the wool blanket I'd used to cover the scratchy cushions. "There's always one of the captain's chairs up front." The RV came equipped with a queen bed in the back. The tiny bench couch and dining table folded down and assembled into a full-size rack that was a bit more comfortable than sleeping on the ground. The chairs in the front swiveled around, so you had extra seating, but other than that, there weren't palatable options.

"But there's no... walls."

She motioned toward the back where Ant was.

"Never needed any before."

Her silence betrayed her thoughts.

"Having second thoughts?" I asked.

Her mouth opened and closed once before she rallied. "Do you always sleep naked?"

For her, I would. "Yeah."

She turned pink.

I had to poke at her a bit. "Do you?"

"Absolutely not."

"Want to?"

When she didn't answer immediately, I knew she was thinking about it. Then she reminded me of her situation.

"I suppose I'll have to, seeing as I don't have any clothes with me."

There was a solution for that. I rummaged in the storage bins and tugged out one of Ant's old shirts. He'd lost so much weight in the last year that I was able to pick him up and carry him. Before that, though, he was a giant. He'd been that way forever. The way he told it, there already was one big guy named "Tiny" in the club, so they named him "Ant."

"Here."

She held the shirt up against her for size and read the design. "*My bike isn't the only thing with gas*? Classy." Her suppressed laughter gave her away, however.

"That's one of the better ones."

"Theo's got one that says, 'My other ride is your mom.' "

"I've seen that one." Hell, I think I owned the same design at one time or another.

"I'll be right back." She slipped into the bathroom to change.

When she came out, she tugged the bottom of the shirt down in an attempt to cover herself, but it wasn't working.

"Lady, I've seen your ass. Why are you so skittish suddenly?"

She froze like a deer in the headlights. "That was different."

Instead of asking her how it was different, I began to strip down, just to even the odds a bit. As I put my pants off to the side, her breath caught.

"Now you've seen *my* ass. Like it?"

"Do I get to touch it?"

I turned to give her a full frontal. "Touch anything you want." My dick agreed wholeheartedly, going from only mildly stiff to full attention.

She looked over her shoulder, listening for Ant's snores. I grabbed my boxers and pulled them back on. "I get it. Not the time, not the place." As much as I wanted it to be the time and place, Betty Jo deserved respect. I intended to show that to her.

"Betty Jo, come here, please?" I sat down on the bed we had to share so she wouldn't feel as intimidated.

She bypassed my arm's reach and stood between my legs. Naturally, I had to feel the tender skin behind her knees. God, she was soft. I ran my fingers along her skin, feeling my way along her curves.

"You and I? We don't know each other very well yet."

"That's an understatement," she shot back.

"I want to." I had to stop what I was doing with because it was too damn distracting. I punctuated my words with a tiny squeeze. I was just about to let go when she reached down and pulled my hands up under the hem of the t-shirt.

My fingers traced the perfect curvature of her hips. My thumbs rested easily in the pocket where her thighs ended. The heat of her skin caught me in a spell, and I couldn't break free. Didn't want to.

She wasn't wearing panties.

"Betty Jo?" My thumbs caressed inwards, drawn to her pussy.

"Yes, Fin."

Not a question but an answer. *Holy shit.*

I brushed between her legs and took my time discovering what made her gasp, what touches triggered clues to my next discovery.

She rocked from side to side to shuffle her stance wider, giving me access to her deeper secrets.

Instead of paying attention to where my fingers were, I watched her face. Noticed when her eyes fluttered closed. What touch made her lips part in a gasp, where my strokes made her moan.

I learned her through her reactions. In doing so, I fell completely and utterly in love with the person she kept hidden under sarcasm and wit. Found out how soft and loving she was deep inside. That beauty wasn't painted on her skin. It was inside her soul.

God, she was made to love.

She opened her eyes and caught herself on my shoulders. "I'm dizzy."

"Yeah?" I motioned to the bed with at tilt of my head, hoping she'd spread her legs wide for me. But no one was a mind reader. "Lay down and open up for me. I want to eat that pussy until you scream."

"Fin!" My dirty talk didn't impress her.

"Please, Betty Jo, please?" I wasn't above begging for a taste of her.

She brushed my hair back and kissed me. "You make me feel beautiful."

"That's because you are. So goddamn beautiful."

"Really?"

Instead of arguing about it, I looked her in the eye and spoke the truth. "Your hair is like the night sky. Your eyes are soft but flash like gems when you're being sarcastic. Your lips, my God, are so damn sweet. I could drink honey wine and not be as satisfied as one taste makes me feel.

"And your skin." I had to bury my face in her stomach to get a good inhale of her scent. I dug my fingertips into her flesh to draw her close. "It's soft like angel wings. I'm drunk on you. And I swear I could never touch a drop of whiskey again without remembering how you make me feel so much higher than it ever could."

I fell onto my back as she kissed me again and again. When I rolled her under me, she arched up, begging me to make her feel drunk, too.

There was only one answer, yes. I helped her take off Ant's ugly shirt. With her breasts exposed, I sucked one and caressed the other, indulging in a fantasy realm of texture from the hard nipple to the smooth ring around it, then the downy soft flesh beyond. Over and over, I tasted and licked from one breast to the other.

But she pushed me lower, spreading her thighs. Opening to me and inviting me to taste heaven.

It was better than that. Frankly, I lost my mind exploring the ways of her.

"Your beard," she gasped.

"What about it?" The taste of her was tangy on my tongue.

"Feels good on my thighs."

She spoke between gulps of air.

To test her reaction, I rubbed my chin against her skin.

Her reaction was a delicious moan. Then she floored me. "I thought I hated beards. Boy, was I wrong."

"Never cutting it." I pushed my tongue against her clit as soon as I got the words out. Then circled it, dipped down to her sweet, wet cunt and back. Over and over, driving her mad—getting soaked and loving the way her legs would tense up when I got her too close.

Then nothing was close enough. She dug her fingers in my hair and begged me to suck on her in *'just, oh, that way, yes, Fin, there, please, please'*—a plea of pleases, and she pulsed so sweetly under my lips.

My heart was racing, and my dick was ready to shoot its load, but I paused to watch her come back to me. Her soft sapphire eyes focused on my face.

"I need you," she whispered.

The questions that bounced around my head were drowned out by the way those words rang in my soul. Being *needed* was more important to me than being loved. I could show all the ways I loved by providing answers and solutions for a need. But ask me to speak the words? I couldn't. My lips would stumble, my tongue fall short of the poetry of my heart. I worked back up her glorious body and kissed her. Showing her that I needed her as much as she needed me.

Her fingers slipped under the band of my boxers, and she stroked my dick. Then she tugged and pulled the elastic until I had to help her remove the interfering bastards. I was two long, mind-blowing strokes in when I realized we were being foolish. "I need a condom."

"No, you don't."

"Sweetheart, I don't want kids." I tried to pull out.

She dug both of her sets of claws into my ass. "Good, because I can't have 'em."

I had to get confirmation before things went any further. "Can't or don't think you can?"

"Can't. I got my tubes tied. My father signed off on it since Roger wouldn't. The damn bastard was ready to kill me just to have a fucking kid."

That warranted a bigger discussion, one that my dick was begging me not to pursue. Of course, part of my brain was on board with putting it off as long as necessary. Not to mention I was already deep inside her and feeling how fucking good it was to be wrapped up in her beautiful body. "Later. We'll talk about that later."

Her eyes met mine. I flexed my hips, going deeper.

"Yeah, later." Her breathy words turned into a moan of pleasure

Aw, hell, yes. All systems go, green lights down the line, and I was ready.

But instead of jack-hammering away like a madman, I slowed down to maintain eye contact with her. This was our first time. Something special and amazing, not something I wanted to rush through and regret because I missed a cue or hurt her feelings by being selfish.

With patience, I stoked her flames. Took time to build up the pace. It was like forging metal. Move too fast, and the pressure breaks the welds. Too little pressure and the bonds didn't form. It took skill to get it just right. That's what I called upon at that moment with her. She was a blade in the making. Worked with skill, she'd be unbreakable and hold an edge all on her own accord. Little effort would be needed to keep her honed to precision. I wanted that.

Someday, I'd be gone, and she'd have to carry on without me. Forged under the right mastery, she'd shine bright. She'd already been hammered too much. It was my turn to warm and temper the spirit inside that begged to be uncovered.

But even the strongest man was weak when the right woman held them. I lost all concept of time and space in her embrace. I broke, melted, reformed, annealed, and found my own reincarnation that night.

Later, at some point between bliss and the demons of night, Ant's muffled pain woke me. I tugged on my jeans and checked on him. He needed help getting out of bed and into the tiny bathroom. I held him up and cleaned him. Dealt with his bitching, and proved I cared by not complaining.

Betty Jo pulled on her pants and the oversized t-shirt and helped me get him comfortable again. She didn't complain, either. Even when Ant tried to embarrass the fuck out of us for having sex within earshot.

"Mind your shit, old man. I can't tell you how many times you woke me up by banging some bitch against your headboard."

"I put the headboard against your wall so you'd get an education, asshole."

"Already had one, you old bastard."

"No, you didn't. You came to my doorstep ignorant and lazy. I put you to work just to make you leave."

"I stayed just to make your life miserable."

"Damn good job of it, too," he wheezed out.

"Fuck you, old man."

That was the way of things between us.

Sarcasm and insults meant "I love you."

Hell, in the Destroyers family, a good fist to the jaw was a way of telling a brother you'd do whatever it took to keep them in the correct highway lane of life. Fights were common. More often than not, you scuffled to settle disagreements. Not one of my brothers lost sleep on words like, "I love you" or "I'm happy to be with my club." Nope, it was asshole this, fucktard that. Every man was called a son of a bitch more often than by his road name.

Getting placed front and center as the butt of jokes was a sign of affection.

Hard slaps on the back and bear hugs so hard you heard your rips creak were the softest touches you could expect. A sock in the arm or a thwack upside the back of your head was, "Hi, how are you?" In the biker world, respect was king, disrespect was love.

You had to worry when it wasn't there.

When men started treating you carefully.

When they stopped caring and cut you out.

Or, when men like Ant didn't shoot the shit with you, that meant there was a problem. I knew Ant's short temper and sharp words meant he had enough energy to put up a fight.

Nights like tonight, those barbed ripostes were in short supply.

As I laid him down in the back, he caught a hand around my neck and tangled a grip in my hair. "Shoot me." He'd begged me to do this before. The answer was still the same.

I sighed. "Ain't gonna shoot you."

"Wish someone would. It fucking hurts." His breathing was shallow, and it took him time to untangle his grip on me.

"I know," I said back, working as carefully as I could to make him comfortable.

"No, you don't. You don't know a damn thing about cancer. It feels like someone stuck rebar up into my joints and froze it, then dumped it into the fire. Everything's jangling and burning and fucking shattering all at once."

Jesus. I could imagine that which sucked. I looked over to Betty Jo, who stopped straightening the new sheet on his bed. Her face had gone pale. Her eyes met mine, and I saw she was feeling it, too.

And she didn't need more pain heaped on her.

"I got it from here."

She shook her head at me. "No, I'll help."

Well, damn. I recognized that determination to be useful. She was like me in too many ways.

Much later, we were back in our bed. I held her in my arms. But neither of us could sleep.

"If I could see the future…" she trailed off.

"We'd have a place somewhere in the country." I could envision it.

"Not here."

"Not anywhere close to California," I agreed.

Her hum of agreement resonated against my skin. I'd take her as far away from the west coast as possible. That got me thinking.

"I was in Maryland a few years back. Big Mike and I stayed in a little log cabin in the middle of nowhere. He fell in love with it so hard, he bought the damn thing." That was only part of the story. The real reason he bought the land would follow me to the grave.

"Mike's the one who shot Pa's roof, right?"

"Yeah." *Bastard.* He started this whole shit show.

"What were you doing in Maryland?"

I took a deep breath and let it out. My hesitation got her attention. It was on the tip of my tongue to lie to her. But for some reason, I couldn't.

"Nothing illegal, I hope?"

"Sweetheart…" I warned her with my tone not to ask any more questions she didn't want to know the answer to.

"Oh."

Yeah, *oh.*

"Maybe not Maryland, then."

I shrugged. "It's as good of a place as any. We didn't get caught at what we weren't supposed to be doing there."

"You didn't?" She propped her chin on her hands and took in my measure.

I stroked down the long trail from her neck to her ass, feeling the beautiful curves and imagining them as a highway I could ride forever. "We were there helping a supporter club. Bunch of good-ol-boys with more balls than brains got in a fight with the Demons out there."

Betty Jo sucked in a breath. She'd likely heard of that club in her time around the Wicked Legion. Not everyone got along. Who got along with who was always shifting and changing and bouncing from war to war. The one between her cousin's club and mine was older than most.

"Mike and I set 'em straight, sorted out their shit."

Her eyebrow went up. "You mean you knocked heads around."

We did things much worse than that. To humor her, I let a little chuckle leak out. "Something like that."

She laid her head to the side and breathed deeply. I thought she'd fallen asleep, but she started talking again. "That cabin, will it fit us, Ant and us?"

It was a tiny little one-bedroom. There was a bathroom not much bigger than the one we had in the RV. But it had a good-sized porch and a view of trees that went on forever. It wouldn't fit all three of us. However, I couldn't see Ant making it through the trip. So, I lied. "For a bit."

I made a mental note to reach out to the chapter out there and see if their president kept up on repairs like he said he would. Maybe I could trade some favors in? Maybe if we took our time, going only a few hours a day and giving him time to rest and shit, we'd have to figure out how to squeeze into that place. Mike owed me. Moreover, I could guard the secrets better on-site than a part-time biker with no skin in the game ever could. That club could give us some protection, too. We wouldn't be flapping in the breeze for our enemies to pick us off like we were on the farm.

As I made plans, I traced the hills and curves of her skin, memorizing the road so I could find my way no matter what came next. Because, plans or not, getting there wasn't going to be an easy ride.

CHAPTER 15

Two days later, we'd traded in my car for a nondescript but ancient truck. Fin dropped a bunch of scratch at Walmart to stock me up, and I settled into their routine fairly well. Ant needed help but insisted he could wipe his own ass, so I let him be as I cleaned the dishes in the sink. As I did, I peeked outside the low window. More RVs had pulled in, and there was constant commotion. Fin was out there directing traffic.

"What is going on?"

"Betty Jo, I'm done. Stick your tits under my arm so I can wash my hands."

"As long as you don't wipe those filthy things on me this time." I was getting used to the old man's antics. Heck, he wasn't much different than my father. All bristle and porcupine on the outside and soft as butter underneath. Once I figured that out, I also figured out that Ant would rather be bitched at than coddled. I made it my life's mission not to curb my words.

I got him sorted and settled on the couch, then peeked out the window again. Fin had disappeared. "Who all is out there?"

"That would be the troupe." Yes, it had an "e" at the end with the way he said it.

"The who?"

"Troupe, you know, actors and crafts persons."

"For what?" There was a brightly colored tent being erected not more than fifteen yards away from the group of trailers that had clustered around ours.

"The faire." With another damn "e."

A man in leggings, complete with a codpiece, strolled past the RV.

"That ain't like any faire I've ever seen."

"Oh, you are in for a treat." Ant sighed and leaned back, resting his head on the stack of pillows Fin placed there for him. "Get my hat, will ya?"

Hat?

"Where is it?"

"In the back closet, you can't miss it."

Sure as shit, there was no missing a massive pirate hat, complete with a three-foot-long ostrich feather. I propped it on Ant's head, then went outside to set the lounge chair up for him because he demanded I take him "out to the sunshine."

He sat like a king on his aluminum and canvas throne. As soon as the word spread that Ant was out and about, folks came by to say hi.

Well, some semblance of "hi." Mostly it wasn't any language I'd ever heard before. It was English, of a sort, but twisted up like a pretzel and slathered with a bunch of flowery tomfoolery.

"Good morn to ye. Tis a blessed morn indeed to be graced with your lordship's presence." The knight, no kidding, a knight, bowed to Ant. "And doubly blessed by your beauty, milady." He bowed deeper.

At first, I was taken aback, but after about the twentieth time hearing it, I smiled and gave a rough curtsy back. These folks were a hoot. There was no mistaking the modern RVs around us, but as the tent city grew larger, the vehicles became a little island of the modern day surrounded by 16th-century Elizabethan England.

Around three, Ant complained about the heat, and I helped him get into bed with the RV's air-conditioner running. He was due for his next medicine dose anyway, so I assisted with that as well. As he rested, I soaked up the cold that seeped into the rest of the vehicle. A person could get used to this.

Life was pretty simple when you only had eight times twenty feet of space. You'd think that it would feel cramped with three people living, eating, and all the other things folks do, but it didn't feel that way, especially since it was a completely different world outside the door.

Fin came back about four—in a rush. "Sorry, I'm back late. Ant's gotta be in pain by now."

"Gave him the meds about an hour ago, flipped on the AC, and let him have a bite or two of the tuna I mixed up for sandwiches. He's sleeping pretty good. I checked on him fifteen minutes ago."

He stood at the top of the steps, mouth open and blinking at me.

"Go, check on him yourself." I motioned to the back.

A hearty snore echoed through the trailer.

Fin's face slowly morphed into a bit less frazzled and a hundred-fold happier. The lines of worry melted like ice under the California sunshine. "You did all that?"

"Yup. Not a complete idiot."

"Betty Jo, don't talk about yourself like that."

I smiled, mostly to myself. *Stick a pin in this, Betty Jo,* I told myself. Fin was one of the good ones. He noticed things, like when someone went and did something to make his life easier. Well, if he thought that was better than gold, then I was the right woman for it. Hell, I'd slaved for over six years, practically killing myself for one back-handed compliment a year from Roger. To get something like that not once but almost constantly from Fin was enough to make my smile wobble.

"What's wrong?"

"You noticed." I swallowed the lump in my throat. The damn bugger popped right back up.

He made a sound of disgust. "Like I'm not supposed to or something?"

That got my attention. The last thing I wanted was to be treated like shit again. Best set him straight early. "Finnigan Curty, you stop being nice to me, and I'll poison your supper."

It wasn't meant to be funny. I was dead serious. But Fin's laughter was contagious. "You do that. I'll just be grateful I didn't have to make supper on top of everything else today."

He sat down beside me with a thump and a sigh. "Don't let me fall asleep."

"You smell like a barn."

"Horses came in."

The more I thought about what he said, the more I didn't understand. "Explain, please? I'm new to this."

His closed eyes opened as he shot me an amused grin. Then they dropped closed again. He looked beat-up and bone-tired. With a huge inhale, then a heavy exhale, he explained.

"There's about thirty men and women here who will re-enact jousting and other medieval events. They brought their horses in and set them up in the barn. There's more than one per person because the heat is pretty hard on the animals. Quite a few of them needed a once-over to make sure they didn't damage anything along the trip. I'm a registered farrier."

"A registered what?"

"Farrier. I can make the shoes and put them on. Found out early on there was a need for one at these things."

I still didn't understand, but he looked so worn out that I let it go. "Are you hungry?"

He grunted, which I took for a yes. But as I stood up, he caught my hand. "I know I smell like a barn. Sorry about that."

His fingers loosened and caressed my skin. Even worn out, he took care to make sure I knew I was treasured.

So I kissed him. Sometimes, it wasn't whether a man was handsome or smelled like the latest expensive cologne; it was who they were inside. I'd take horse shit over asshole any day of the week.

"That's what I needed." He smiled with his eyes closed. His hand dropped to his side with a plop.

"You need a shower and food. And rest."

"Can't. They're setting up the—"

I put a finger over his lips. "You are going to rest. Ant is taken care of, and those other folks gotta wait in line. Understood?"

One eye popped open. "You bossing me around?"

"Yup. Get used to it."

His chest shook with silent laughter. "Or you'll poison my food."

"You betcha."

This time, I was teasing.

Later that evening, Fin took me around the grounds. Grand opening was at noon the next day, but everything was in place. The players and tradespersons gathered around a stage. Some generous soul passed out cups of honey mead, and I got my first taste.

To say it was love at first sip is an understatement.

"Why isn't this for sale everywhere?" I held up my second cup, now almost empty.

"Because it's too easy to get drunk on." Fin nudged me with his shoulder. "Speaking of, how you feeling?"

"Drunk, but not drunk-drunk." Even then, I slurred my words. I eyeballed the glass. "Funny, I don't get this bad on two beers."

"Sweetheart, this is like five or six beers." Fin took my cup and drank down the last of it.

I complained, of course. My words bounced right off him.

A shout rose up from the front of the audience. I craned my head to see what was going on. A minstrel read from a long piece of parchment. But he kept his words brief.

"Hear ye, good ladies and lords of the court. On yon morrow, we toil."

The crowd booed. I booed along, not really understanding everything.

"But to this night, we hail!"

The crowd shouted.

Beside me, Fin bellowed out, "Huzzah!"

"Say it once, say it trice …" He lifted a drinking horn into the air.

I joined in by the second "Huzzah!" By the third, I wanted nothing more than to scream "Huzzah" to the stars, fully bought into the fun.

"Drink, eat, make merry."

Fin handed me his cup so I could take a drink with everyone else. Someone in the crowd yelled for the players. But the guy up front claimed they were far too drunk, only in more flowery words than I could follow. Then a chant went up for a play.

Drunk Shakespeare was hilarious. Even more so, when Fin ran onto the stage and picked up the donkey head the player dropped and began to chase the prettiest actor around. He, the actor, not Fin, was not amused. But the rest of us were.

Fin handed the ass head to someone else, claiming he didn't know the words, and joined me. A woman plunked herself next to me and addressed him. "Is this your wench?"

I gave her my best stink-eye.

Fin dropped an arm over my shoulders and leaned around me to say, yes, I was.

I poked him for that.

"Peace, woman. A wench is any marriageable lady who isn't royalty."

"Proud wench here." The woman pointed at her boobs, pushed up by a super tight corset. She had more on display than I possessed. For a moment, I marveled at the audacity. Then realized wench and bitch were probably sides of the same coin.

"Wench, huh?"

"A beautiful, bounteous wench. Thou takest mine breath." Fin smacked his lips on my cheek.

The woman leaned in, "I know it is a costume optional tonight, but I bet you would make a lovely lady of the court. Unless you're dressing as a smithy wife tomorrow."

Costume? Somehow I doubted the local Walmart carried what I needed to fit in around this crowd. The mead I'd drank soured in my stomach. Fin was in his costume. Brown homespun pants and a simple cream-colored shirt that was super soft to the touch. He'd put it on after taking a good long shower to wash off the horse barn odors.

"About that, you feel like opening a bit early so I can get her a few outfits?" Fin leaned in, sandwiching me between them as they canoodled about my clothing.

"You're a vendor here?" I interrupted. She looked more like one of the actors.

"Oh, Mistress Smithy, I am wounded by thee. Forsooth, no mere vendor art myself. Thou partaketh company of the finest dress merchant at this humble faire."

I shot Fin a look, asking, "She's laying it on thick, isn't she?"

"Thick or thin, thou canst do wrong with finery befitting thine status. Thou art the rarest gem." He switched from character to ask her point blank. "What you got for a lady of the court?"

"Lady?"

He looked me dead in the eye and corrected me.

"I'd have you be the queen, but it isn't my say."

"Oh-ho, 'tis like that?" she interjected.

"Absolutely like that," Fin replied.

Our visitor speculated for a moment, then asked, "Did you know that the Smith's wife was likely the richest woman in town?"

One look at Fin and I burst out laughing. "Really?"

He crossed both arms over his chest with a frown. One corner of his lips quirked up, though, because he didn't know what was coming but knew me well enough to suspect I was up to something. I was. The years of hanging around with cheap-ass bikers taught me one thing that stuck hard. Haggling was serious business. But there wasn't any fun in life if you couldn't haggle like your life depended on it.

If Fin had his way, the woman would sell me the most extravagant thing in her shop, probably at a cutthroat rate, leaving poor Fin and Ant a lot poorer. But that wasn't going to happen on my watch. And to save Fin from himself, I had to play this carefully. He'd pay whatever it took to make me the finest lady here, but I didn't need that. Give me a mug of honey mead and a linen sack, and I'd be content. *Or maybe that was the booze talking?*

She didn't know my thoughts, though. That meant I needed to get a great deal but not ruin Fin's reputation. And, not let on that I was being cheap.

In the pause, Fin took his cup back from me and brought it to his lips. I waited until he was mid-sip.

"Maybe his wife is rich, but you're only looking at the wench he's fucking."

Mead shot out of his nose and soaked his beard. He coughed and bent over to catch his breath. I slapped his back as I began the haggling.

"What would his mistress wear?"

One hour later, I was in a pitch-dark tent, dressed in finely embroidered silk. The undergarment was even softer than Fin's good shirt. The shoes were hand-crafted lambskin. The soles were double-thick hide, and the edges had real ermine trim. Just the material for the shoes alone was well over a hundred dollars. Yet Fin handed over a single fifty along with a promise to bring a yard of silver chain in trade.

As we walked together under the stars, he took my hand. Not in the usual grab-and-swing way, but tenderly. Holding it lifted between his two hands as if I were something precious.

Men and women alike bowed or curtsied as they gamboled past.

When we reached the trailer, he held the door for me. "My lady."

I paused. "Did I do good?"

He snorted. "She's been begging for silver from me for years. I was going to give it to her for free, but glad to see I got a good trade for it."

I couldn't tell if he was upset or happy. "The shoes are about three-fifty in a good market. The dress probably four hundred. How much was the chain worth?"

His mouth hung open. "Maybe two hundred."

"A good trade then." I dipped my head to him and proceeded up the stairs.

"Whoo-ee, who looks like a million bucks?" Ant whistled or tried to. He was too high to purse his lips. Pot crumbs littered the table, and the trailer smelled like a brush fire.

"Are you stoned?" Fin asked.

"Hell yeah." Ant swayed in his seat.

"That can't be good with his meds," I commented.

Fin grimaced. His skin flushed red, and I would bet my brand new shoes he was angry as fuck. I expected him to rip Ant a new asshole.

"Where'd you get it?" he calmly asked instead.

Ant leaned back. "I ain't sharing if that's what you're asking."

"There it is," Fin muttered, then sighed. "You hungry, old man?"

"Hell yeah. Got some Doritos?"

Fin pulled the bag down from the cabinet. In the meantime, I gathered up the shake and put it back onto the little tray with his rolling papers. Then chased after the crumbs Ant littered everywhere.

"Good woman you got here, Fin. Pretty tits, too." He leaned in, and the top of his head brushed my arm. Luckily, he missed my tits. As angry as Fin was, I wouldn't put it past him to teach Ant a lesson over it.

"Up you go, Ant. Time for bed," Fin said.

"Whoa, I wasn't done." He leaned sideways, unable to get his feet under him. I took the other side, and we managed to get him through the RV to the back, where Fin insisted he had things under control.

"Damn fine tits. I wanna take a bite of 'em."

That was my cue to leave Fin to it. I slipped into the tiny bathroom to change.

He'd put up with a lot today. Hopefully, between the pot and the meds, Ant would sleep well, and we'd have a bit of time to ourselves before things got crazy tomorrow.

I took care to remove the outer gown and tie off the undergarment with a belt before heating up some soup for Ant. Hopefully, he'd let me feed him, and we'd be spared a mess to clean up.

"That for Ant?"

Fin came up behind me and wrapped his arms around me. The thin chemise was barely a barrier, and his hands made me shiver with anticipation. "Figured he might eat some between chips."

"I'll take it back to him. You wait here."

"I can handle it." I turned toward him.

He frowned. "You probably could, but…" his eyes dipped south, drawing my gaze down.

Hell. The thing was practically see-through. "Oh."

"Looks good on you." His eyes fixed on the spot where my nipples were. The hard tips plainly visible despite the fabric.

I gathered up both and squeezed them up, mimicking what a corset would do. "I don't know. Maybe I need a corset."

Without the structure of the dress, the neckline of the linen was daringly low.

Fin's breath let out in a whoosh of utter shock.

Poor man.

"Feed Ant. I'll set up the bed. Then you can get more than just a look."

That got him moving.

CHAPTER 16

Things fell into place almost too easily. I'd been worrying how I was going to handle sales while I gave demonstrations, but with Betty Jo along, I was able to focus on what I did best, hammering and yammering about it. The kids ate it up, and the adults were just as curious.

With each new question, I was taken back to the day I stood in those shoes. And I'd answer in the same gruff way Ant answered my peppered questions. I'd spent at least half my life hearing him talk and watching him teach the same things over and over. But despite all those years, there was always something new to learn. Something that only comes from years of pounding out a rhythm of steel on steel.

Now it was my turn to tell the secrets I'd discovered.

The bonds of brotherhood surpassed words. Life pressed each layer of knowledge into the layers folded down before. We'd worked side-by-side, Ant and me. As I talked, I imagined his gruff corrections and tempered my words to pay homage to the history and pass as much of it down as I could.

During a lull, I glanced over at Betty Jo. Her laughter made me smile. She didn't hide her enjoyment. Instead, she threw her whole body into it with gusto. I wanted to bear witness to that joy forever. In order for that to happen, we needed to get shot of California.

Easier said than done with Ant getting worse each day.

I suspected he was buying more than pot. We'd been here for almost four weeks, and the faire was closing up shop after tonight's joust. Whatever he was buying, it wasn't good. It sucked up his life faster than the energy it gave him. He'd dropped weight and was cranky as shit when it wore off. When it got too bad, he'd beg me to kill him.

More than once, Betty Jo cried herself to sleep because of his pleas. I wanted to join her, but someone needed to carry the burden. So, my eyes stayed dry as I cleaned him up and pretended there was no change in his health. But one of these days, I'd have to stop denying the inevitable. That, I dreaded more than the bitching. Every time I closed up the forge, I glanced to the post where I had hung his knife and reminded myself that I'd enjoy any time with Ant above ground that remained. Even the bad times, the drugged-up lost hours, and the twice-nightly trips to the back of the trailer to check on him.

But that was a few hours from now. Meanwhile, I needed to take care of my future and the woman I intended to spend it with. There was a lull as the crowds moved on to the minstrel show.

"Hey, Betty Jo, you hungry?"

"I'm good."

She wasn't. She hadn't eaten in a bit, and I worried about her as well.

I'd asked the traveling nurse about diabetes, particularly how we could keep it at bay. Turkey legs were surprisingly acceptable, along with Betty Jo's salads and whole grains.

"Well, I'm hungry," I grumbled.

"You're always hungry." She scanned the crowd just like a seasoned veteran of the festival circuit does. It clicked that she'd do that with her years of helping her father.

I snuck behind her and brushed a kiss on her neck, being certain to make my beard tickle her skin.

"Fin!" She ducked her head and spun around to glare at me.

"I'm hungry for you, wench."

"Methinks thou art a rogue."

I was and planned on continuing to be one from birth to death and told her as much. She caught on to the lingo like a natural. Give her another couple of weeks, and they'd crown her queen.

"Come with me. I want a turkey leg."

"You don't need me with."

"Please?"

Her eyebrow shot up, making a perfect bend. I wanted to copy that shape and create a hilt with just that precise transition from line to curve.

"Who's gonna watch the shop?"

"No one. That's what the sign is for." I propped said board up on the fence surrounding the clearing where I did the demonstrations and then secured the gate.

"But the turkey vendor is all the way on the other side."

"Think of it as exercise, woman."

Her complaining lasted until I tugged her behind a tapestry. The noise of the crowd dimmed in the little grove of campers and tents the employees set up for easy access. A few folks, performers like us, milled around, resting between shows in the shade. Betty Jo and I greeted each by name when we could.

On the other side, it was a quick walk to the food stalls. A juggler entertained the crowd in line. Some patrons were dressed up fancier than the players here, earning them the nickname of "playtrons." Most wore hodgepodge assembled outfits that ranged from pirate to elf, with the almost steady parade of wizards or magic users in between. There were a few with good armor on. One in particular stood out. I stopped to ask a few questions about where it came from because I couldn't peg the artisan. Information like that was important. One day I'd have a forge I could make armor with. I wanted to collect names so I could visit and learn their techniques. Maybe after Ant passed on, I'd add to the barn... *Damn*. My predicament hit home. We weren't going back to the farm after this. Not with me supposedly dead and Betty Jo on the run like she was.

"You okay?" Betty Jo studied my face.

"Got thinking."

"About?"

"Nothing but future problems. They can wait." I brushed a curl away from her face and let my fingers linger on her soft skin. It was my favorite way to pass the time, touching her.

At the mention of our future, her smile fell, and she heaved a sigh. "Can we forget real life and do this forever?"

I looked around. There was steady business to be had accommodating the people who wanted to pretend for a weekend or five every year. The juggler was a regular fixture on the circuit. He spent whole months traveling with fires like these or working private events and parties. Sometimes, he busked on the streets. It wasn't ever going to make him rich, but the happiness he found in the life couldn't be bought.

With Betty Jo at my side, it might be a good life for me, too.

"I'm down with that."

She beamed. It was a sight to behold.

"Hail, Master Smithy, prithee a meet?"

While there wasn't one set leader in charge, the man hailing me did his best to wrangle the parade of misfits around here. I assembled my "nice" face despite wanting to get a damn turkey leg and disappear into some shade with Betty Jo for an hour or more.

"Well, met milord." I lowered my tone as he moved closer. "What's up?"

He greeted Betty Jo with a proper bow, a "milady," and a kiss to the back of the hand. "Your partner is most beautiful. Methinks thou art endowed with the fairies' own luck."

"He's endowed alright," Betty Jo quipped back.

"Ho! Bawdy wench." His guffaw drew attention.

I gave Betty Jo a squeeze so she could feel the laughter I was trying to keep inside.

Betty Jo curtsied prettily.

When the jests died down, and the line's attention moved on, I asked him what he wanted.

"I was wondering if Master Ant is up for an appearance this afternoon?"

The smile fell from my face. "He's doing worse." The heat was hard on him. Being in the middle of chaparral country spared us the extremes of the desert just beyond the San Bernardino and San Gabriel ranges. But it was still too much for him.

The player frowned. "We were hoping to crown him king of the faire today. In appreciation for everything he's done."

I shook my head. Even if Ant was well enough to sit in the sun for the hour or more it took for the joust, he would grouse the entire time about the fuss being made over him. Not knowing what he took while we were busy here made the whole idea a crap shoot that was loaded against us.

"Maybe Lord of the Revels tonight," I offered instead. That was more Ant's speed, and he'd be spared having to sit on the uncomfortable wooden chairs they used as thrones. And we'd have a few hours to let him sleep the drugs out of his system before dosing him up on the right stuff and carting him there.

My suggestion was met with a slap on the back and an order to bring him to the clearing after the faire closed for the week.

He strutted away, leaving Betty Jo and me staring at his back.

"You sure he's up for that?" Betty Jo asked.

"Whether he is or isn't, I think he'll enjoy it." Even stoned out of his mind, Ant loved a party.

I studied her frown. "What?"

"We're both going to have to stay sober tonight to deal with him."

Knowing how out of control Ant could get, she was right about us needing to be sober. He'd be a handful. "Is that okay with you? No honey mead."

As much as she loved the stuff, she kept her intake to a modest two cups. To keep busy, she played hostess most nights. Strategically, she placed herself in the center of the party but kept both hands busy so she wouldn't drink to excess. People loved her, thought her quite the reveler. But she usually stayed in control of any situation. Quite the trick, if you asked me.

"I'll deal. You can't party every day." She looked me in the eye and smiled. A quick wink told me she was on board with the plan. Then her expression faltered. To compensate, she brushed my beard with her hands, and her fingers curled in deep to graze my skin. Unspoken was the worry that hounded us both. Losing her father had been rough on her, but now losing Ant on top of that was eating at her spirit.

I leaned into her touch and rested my hands on her hips. "You've been a rock for us. I appreciate it."

Her fingers tightened to tug me closer. Fixing me in place with her eyes, she spoke, punctuating each word with a little pressure, "Any. Damn. Time. It's nice that you notice. I appreciate that, Master Smith." She gave my head a shake and then kissed me. I gathered her close to deepen the kiss. My tongue slipped inside her mouth, and I lost my worries in her taste.

Things like that don't go unnoticed, especially around folks who make a living off of acting the fool. Someone in the crowd cracked a joke. It was followed by twenty more.

We ducked under another tapestry to escape the teasing. I backed Betty Jo against an ancient sycamore tree. There I could kiss her as deeply as I wanted.

Her skin smelled like salt and sunshine. There was a hazy residue of forge smoke and melting steel that clung to her hair. In other words, she smelled like me. I'd put my stamp on her in scent and in light touches. My lips trailed down her neck to trace the edge of her chemise and slide over the mounds of her breasts. There were three little freckles that had appeared with her tan. I licked each one and sucked on the paler skin exposed when I untied the little bow in the front.

The gaping fabric bunched above her corset but allowed me access to her tits. I took my time, gently paying homage to her beauty with each drag of teeth and swirl of my tongue.

The reward was her groans of pleasure and the increased speed of her breath.

A woman like her was made to worship. I dropped to my knees and slipped my hands under her hem. As I looked up at her face, the sun haloed her dark hair. Giving me a glimpse into heaven.

She took my breath away. I had no words to tell her how gorgeous she was. I fell back on the lines of a play to put the thoughts of my heart into meaning.

"It is the east, and Juliet is the sun."

Betty Jo put a finger on my lips. "Don't."

"Can't help it. You're the most beautiful woman I've ever met."

Her lips tucked in as she held back tears. "Can't say you're the prettiest man I ever met, but you've got the best heart. That is worth so much more than what's on the outside, Fin."

"A pretty face can hide a treacherous soul." I'd heard that somewhere.

Maybe it was the wrong thing to say. Her smile dropped, and her face went cold. "Been there and lived that life."

I squeezed the soft spot at the top of her calves to remind her I wasn't her damned ex-husband.

And like the sun slipping from the clouds, her face lit up. "I love you, Fin."

My mouth went dry. I swallowed to get enough courage to say the words back. But they caught in my mouth. I stammered something stupid instead. "I don't know why."

She dropped to the ground beside me and wrapped her arms around my head. I fell into her lap with a sob. The shit I'd been holding inside for so long bubbled out against her skirt. I clung to her legs, making a mess of the moment. Words I'd long buried spewed forth like a dam breaking.

"My parents hated me."

"I'm sure they didn't." Her fingers threaded through my hair.

"They did. Dad especially. When I found Ant, I…" my throat caught.

Her fingernails dug into my scalp, reminding me with a slight nudge of pain that he wasn't dead yet.

"I thought if I ran away from them, I could have a better life. Or scare them into loving me and hauling me back. They didn't even try to find me. So, I stuck with Ant. I didn't have any place else to go. That cut hard." I let go of the secrets I'd stuffed down deep for over twenty years.

"And the pain never got better. At least it didn't get worse."

She smoothed out the lines on my forehead, combed through my hair, and stroked my beard. "But you stayed with Ant even after that."

I made a noise to agree with her. "For a while, I did everything I could to fit into his shoes. Didn't work."

"No?"

I shook my head. "That pain? It made me angry. Ant was all about the party. I couldn't live like that. Too much shit inside."

"You don't seem angry now."

How could I explain it to her?

"What I did was take it out on others. That made it better and worse. Kind of like feeding a wild wolf. It just makes them hunger for more. I'm not a good man."

"Yes, you are."

I laughed bitterly. The evil I'd done in pursuit of fitting into the Destroyers' world flashed through my head. I'd been so exceptionally good at being bad. "Maybe when Ant passes, I'll leave it behind."

"Leave what?"

"The biker shit."

Her hand stopped stroking. "Why would you do that?"

I'd expected agreement. To hear her sharp question made me search her face.

"Isn't that what you want?"

She stood up so quickly my head dumped onto a tree root.

"Ow!"

My pain was drowned out by her growl of exasperation. "Stupid man!"

I sat up, ready to catch her if she bolted, but utterly confused. "Don't you want out of the life?"

She stood with her arms crossed at her chest, covering up those magnificent tits of hers. "I do."

There was dead grass on my pants, so I brushed it off and thought through things. "So, what's the problem with me saying what I said?"

Betty Jo whirled on me so fast her skirts didn't have time to catch up, and they caused her to stumble a bit, which stopped her from yelling at me. Then she gathered up her emotions and laid out her argument.

"I may want out, but I know you. I know how much you rely on your friends. On *Ant's* friends. *They* are your family. I don't have that. My own cousin would sell me out in a heartbeat. Pa was what kept me around them. *He* was loyal to them. And they killed him anyway!" She didn't stop there, so I didn't have time to digest the vitriol behind her words.

"Hell, you were just saying how your own family hated you. Instead, you found people who didn't. I'd be a horrible bitch to take you away from that."

"You ain't a bitch."

Her open-mouthed and blinking shock that morphed into denial dared me to take the words back.

But I doubled down. "You ain't a bitch. You're one of the most selfless women I've ever met." I meant every damn word of it.

"That's better than hearing, 'I love you.'" Her voice broke on the last three words.

I stood up and gathered her in my arms. "I do, though. I love—" Damn it. I couldn't get it out without choking. I cleared my throat and spoke each word carefully. "I love you, Betty Jo. *You.*"

"You're a damn fool."

That was more our speed.

I chuckled and dipped my head so I could rest it on her shoulder. She grabbed onto my head and held tight. Her quiet sniffles gave her away.

I'd touched something deep inside her. A raw nerve she hadn't guarded well enough. One I intended to nurture and care for until it wasn't painful anymore. She deserved that much—and more.

CHAPTER 17

Fin didn't know me well at all.

Or maybe he did. I was so confused. Hearing him say I was his rock undid all the walls I'd put up. It was something I didn't hear enough of in my life.

Except from my father, who tried to escape the biker life that surrounded him, and it got him killed. A chill slithered down my spine. Call it a premonition, or only common sense, but I knew whatever Fin had done for the Destroyers would make it near impossible for him to just "leave." No one left. They died wearing the colors inked on their skin. I knew that despite not being a member. And the Destroyers were no different than the one who'd killed my father. In fact, I'd bet they were worse. I'd heard stories. Long, evil descriptions of men stripped of their patches for deserting their brothers. Especially the marks tattooed into their skin. No sacrifice was sufficient to get a free pass to freedom.

I was scared for Fin.

Lurking in his eyes were secrets. I saw them clearly when they surfaced.

The tell-tale hesitation in Fin's speech as he declared his love also gave him away. The man in my arms loved deeply. So much so he couldn't put it into words for fear they'd be turned against him. My own father had been such a man. After Mom left us, he endured a dark time. He bought his retirement through whatever Devil's deal he could, but they didn't let him go. He may have been out, but the club never forgot him. Or forgave him for trying to leave. There was no quitting the club. That knowledge placed a cautious pause between the heart and the throat. It took years before the hesitation between words disappeared.

I kissed Fin's brow, savoring the taste of his skin on my lips.

His fingers tightened, and he slipped his hands lower to squeeze my ass.

"You're quite a woman, Betty Jo."

"Shut up and lift my skirt, would you?" After all, we'd just said some stupid shit. Wasn't fucking the next step?

He leaned back to check my intentions.

I sent back as sultry of a reply I could put into my expression.

"Quite a woman." He kissed me, putting hunger into each dominating stroke of his tongue and each ferocious slide of his lips on mine.

My legs caught a breeze as he slid my dress up.

I shuffled to lean against the tree so he wouldn't have to hold me up once my legs turned to jelly—and they would. Every time we made love, my body yearned for more and, in the reaching, gave its everything to crawl up into our fucking and never ever leave.

With one leg wrapped around his ass, I tilted my legs open so he could slide in and out. Sweat broke out on his brow, and I smeared it away and kissed him harder.

He rocked deep, angling upward with a dip of his knees and lifting me with each heave of passion.

Fin was strong in a deceivingly wiry way. Years of hammering metal into shape gave him a physique that didn't tire. It was a match for the efforts I gave back to him. Pulling him closer, I clawed at his back as we strove for the right pinnacle of heat that would drive us over the edge.

The faire, Ant, fleeing my home, it all swept away when we made love. All that was left was the slight space between strokes where we'd breathe hurriedly into the void and crash together again as we searched for the right fit.

"We're forge welded, Betty Jo," he gasped. "Heat binds the metal together, even if it shouldn't bond naturally."

I squeezed tight, making the bond closer. "Harder, Fin. Harder." I imagined his hammer tapping down on the hot metal and married the rhythm in my head to the thrust of his hips. My body quivered from the emotions surging inside me. "I love you," I repeated myself to make sure he knew someone out there loved him beyond life, beyond trouble, and beyond all the heartbreak the world held.

With a groan, he emptied inside me, and the beat quieted. With the same grace he used to lay his hammer down, he slid his hand up my thigh to cup my ass. "Love you, too." His beard scraped my neck as he hid against my skin. I clutched his hair as I tried to catch my breath.

While the corset I wore with this dress was pretty, it was also damn confining. My heart beat so quickly it made me weak. A bead of sweat slid down my neck to roll over my breast and tickle the underside. The breeze blew across my exposed nipple and brought me back to the real world.

The noises of the faire lingered beyond the hedge of tapestries and wooden walls. We were damn lucky no curious guests peeked in on us. "I'm hungry now. Let's get that turkey leg." I pushed at him so I could fix my dress.

Fin was as bad as Pa, feeding me all the time. I knew, deep down, it was just another way to say, "I love you." As long as it wasn't controlling or unkind, I embraced the deed but still had to put my own stamp of love on top of it. Fin rarely did sweet. Nor did he trust it. Therefore, it was best to poke at him any chance I got.

His shoulders shook with laughter, and he helped me get my dress tucked back into propriety. I brushed the grass off of his ass and redid the ponytail that kept his hair from catching fire from a stray spark. Then, I stopped to brush the perspiration from his skin.

"You're amazing." I had to sneak at least one compliment in there.

"So are you, my Juliet."

That damn chill was back. I shook my head. "I keep telling you—you're getting it wrong."

"I know. They die. Everybody dies, Betty Jo. Eventually, happy ever afters end." He sighed and his shoulders bent slightly as if the weight he carried settled back into place.

Maybe he was talking about us, or maybe dwelling on his life with Ant.

A crease formed between his eyebrows. I brushed at it, but it didn't quite go away. "Then we gotta make sure the days between are good, right?"

He nodded once, closing his eyes and affirming that he'd do his damnedest to make certain of that.

I traced the edges of his face and let him know how much I appreciated him. "Even if I tease the shit out of you, please know that you are the best man I've ever met. And that includes my father. Maybe you two are tied in my heart, but he's gone, and you're not. So, I'm going to tell you every day how much I love you."

Fin kissed my forehead and held me still as he rubbed his beard across my skin. "Every day. I could live with that." His huff of air fluffed the hair by my ear, and I snuggled into his body to keep him close for just a moment longer.

The moment slipped away. Fin held me out at arm's length and tilted his head. "Your father—was he a good man?"

"The best, and no not good at all." I'd heard so many stories about the days before he met my mother. She was no angel, being one of those women who chased bikers to land herself an old man. Trouble was, she couldn't handle it once she had and split. Her loss.

Fin smiled lopsidedly. "I can understand that."

"He killed for the club." I shouldn't tell him a secret like that, but I needed him to know how deep the lifestyle was ingrained in my soul.

The smile fell from Fin's face. At that moment, I knew Fin had done the same. But it didn't matter.

"I heard the story when I was five, about a year before Mom left."

He waited to see if I'd elaborate. When I didn't, he kissed me on the forehead, giving me that secret to keep. "I gave up the club life when Ant moved out here. My nomad status gives me leeway to do my own thing. It's possible we won't have to deal with a bunch of idiots up our asses once we get on the road. But I can't make promises." His head dipped eastward, indicating which direction we'd head once the faire wrapped up.

I took a deep breath to fortify the walls. I'd fallen deep for a biker. Again.

"You are getting help to pack up the forge, aren't you?" Two could play the 'ignore the elephant' game.

Fin nodded. "Probably should start on that early. Then we'll get Ant set up for the party tonight." His fingers lingered on my skin. "We'll take the trip slow. Maybe we could stay here another day or two so he can rest."

I smiled because it seemed like the right reply. But I really wanted to leave as soon as possible. During the weeks of the faire, there was a fantastical layer of protection wrapped around us. We'd slipped into the world here and successfully hid ourselves from the harsh reality of being right smack dab in the middle of Wicked Legion territory. Without the faire community, we would soon be stripped bare. I didn't like that feeling.

But for Ant, we'd have to do it the way Fin proposed. The trip was killing him. It was on the tip of my tongue to tell Fin that we should go back to the farm to make Ant comfortable. But that was a stupid idea. We were no safer there than here. Safety was somewhere east, where the Wicked Legion weren't.

At sunset, a cannon shot signaled the end of the festivities. The crowd shuffled away, sunburnt and satisfied. Fin packed up the forge. It took two of the stronger knights to help him move the anvil into the trailer.

I packed up the stand. In the weeks here, it had become mine, just like the displays my father and I set up. I organized the unsold goods, locked up the money from the stuff that had, and kept an account of the inventory we'd need to replace. *We.* I shook my head at how easily the word slipped into my thinking.

A craftsman stopped by while I was moving a box of wooden swords to the stack of items we needed to fit into the trailer.

"Fin asked me to drop this off before we left." He held a big plastic bin in his hands. Inside, I groaned. More shit to move. The smile I plastered on felt fake.

"What's inside?"

The vendor smiled with a wink. "It's for you. Open it." He set it on the table I'd just cleared.

I glanced at Fin, who was terribly busy directing the packing of the trailer. But got no answers there.

"He said you work leather. I had an old kit to spare and some scraps." Not waiting for me to lift the lid, he flipped the bin open.

I gasped. Inside was leather and fur of all colors and varieties. Even better was a full set of tools, needles, and sinew. "This is…" Amazing, too much, kind beyond words… I couldn't speak.

"It's yours, milady." He left with a little bobbing bow and a fingertip to his cap.

I pulled a couple of layers of material out so I could inventory the gift. It would help me make at least a dozen items. I could picture them in my head. The smell of tanned hide and the supple texture flipped a switch inside me. This was *exactly* what I needed.

Fin paused to look my way, his hands resting on his hips. "You like?" he yelled across the distance.

"I love it. Thank you."

His fingers went to his brow as if to tip a cap at me. Then he went right back to work.

I shook my head at the emotions I felt but paused to rub my hand over my chest to clear the tightness in my throat and the sweet pangs of joy in my heart. Fin was such a decent man. There might not be flowery words or fancy dates, but I'd take the useful, thoughtful things over superficial gestures any day of the week.

The lid went back on the box, and I stacked it with the rest of the items we'd take to the next faire or wherever the road took us.

Back at the trailer, the whole place reeked of pot. I opened the windows to air it out, so Fin wouldn't have to smell it when he got back. Then kept busy cleaning up after the mess Ant made. "Didn't that nurse do anything?" I grumbled as I found yet another beer can littering the floor. The contents spilled out and made the floor under the little booth table ugly sticky. I dug into the under-sink cabinet to drag out the bleach.

The trailer rocked as Fin entered.

"Ain't that the prettiest sight."

I glared at him over my shoulder. "What?"

"Your ass in the air, that's what."

My middle finger went up out of habit.

He laughed and dropped into the booth with a heavy sigh. He set a crude metal knife onto the ledge of the booth. "Is Ant sleeping?"

"He's stoned out of his fucking mind. So maybe. Move your feet." I shooed him around the booth to the other side, then bitched at him to take his shoes off so I could have a clean floor.

"What crawled up your hide?"

"He ain't supposed to be drinking. You heard the nurse. Yet there's beer cans stuffed everywhere except the god-damned waste bin for recycling." I pointed with my sponge at the cabinet where we kept the two bins.

Fin's forehead crunched up. "Who brought him beer?"

"The fuck if I know. Maybe that stupid nurse."

Fin stared at the door, confused. "She wouldn't, would she?"

I sat on my knees and held both hands out with a "Who else do you see around here?" question on my face. "Between that and the pot, I don't know what's going to kill him faster."

As I sat there, tears clouded my vision. I was tired. The day had been long. The night was promising to be longer still, and there wasn't enough good right now to make a dent in the pity party I was pitching in my head.

"Hey," Fin was right there, on the floor, holding me and making soothing noises in my ear.

But like clockwork, a groan of pain made us both freeze.

I couldn't help the whimper of defeat that escaped.

Fin's head tipped to meet mine, and I could feel his pain as keenly as my own. I set down the sponge and wiped my hand on my shorts to dry it before squeezing the tension that gathered around his shoulders. He sighed in brief relief until another moan broke us apart. "I got him. You finish here, okay?"

His work was going to be harder than mine, so I kissed him. "I'll get clean sheets."

We were late to the party, but Ant was all smiles despite the twinges of pain clouding his eyes. For each ale passed his way, Fin intercepted it and handed it off to me to pass along to some grateful sot.

A pretty girl placed a flower garland on Ant's head and kissed his cheek. He slipped his hand up her leg and groped her ass. She laughed it off, thankfully. I met Fin's eyes over the chaos. Unspoken words tossed between us. I shrugged at the question he asked and sent him love back through a small smile. His eyes went soft, and he closed them briefly, as if storing that love down deep. I made certain more was there when his eyes opened. That made him grin. His shoulders straightened, and he joined the merry circle around his mentor and father figure.

For my part, I hung back and took care of the edges, so Fin could enjoy himself. But in the shadows, I watched the crowd to see if someone slipped Ant anything or tried to make contact. Most everyone would be gone in the morning, and I wanted to figure out who was dealing to Ant.

Fin and I ruled out the nurse as she wasn't connected to the world we left. While cleaning, I'd also found the note she left us, warning us not to let him drink, and an emergency number in case we needed it. That meant it was someone from the faire. But there were no signs of any deals going down.

That night, Ant slept straight through. And the next day, Fin got up early to get the rest of the smithy packed away. I hummed along with the radio as I wiped down the dishes from breakfast. It was a great morning, quiet in our little section of the campground. The crowds were gone, and most of the faire folk departed. It was peaceful, and I could finally see the lake again from the little windows above the table. I leaned over to watch a motorboat buzz past. The thing had a loud motor, announcing to the world that the owner was trying to compensate for all the shortcomings of their life. They swept back and forth, making waves and noise just because they could.

I smiled despite the annoyance. With luck, we'd get on the road today. We'd already completed the work of unhooking things and shutting everything down, so Fin could hook up the trailer to the camper once he finished. All we needed were a few good hours of daylight, and we'd be far away from this place.

The RV door opened, and I felt the familiar rocking of the unit as Fin came up the stairs.

"Did you forget something?" I turned to give him a smile and maybe grab a quick kiss before he was gone again.

But it wasn't Fin.

CHAPTER 18

"Well, well, well, you look good for a dead man." Big Mike slapped me on the back, almost knocking me over. I was almost done packing the trailer. Once I got the last of it into the unit, I would go back to Betty Jo and Ant and, with luck, get on the road before noon. Worst-case scenario, we'd rest up for the rest of the day and get some fishing in if that idiot buzzing the lake quit scaring everything into hiding.

But all those plans went to shit because there was no reason for Big Mike to be so deep in enemy territory. "What the fuck you doing here?"

"Visiting."

That was a damn lie. I could read it on his face. "You lie for shit."

Big Mike scanned the grounds. There were very few people left. Those that were around were too busy to notice anything beyond their nose. He stepped in. "I got news."

"I ain't got all day to play games. What do you got?"

"Skirmishes up and down the state line. Wicked Legion crossed over into Nevada last week, burned down a couple of businesses."

"Not just mine, huh?"

Mike shook his head. "And here you are deep in their heartland. Do you have a fucking death wish or something?"

I smiled. "Best place to hide is right in plain sight."

"No, it ain't. You need to get the fuck out of here, like now."

I pointed to the piles of metal I still had to fit in the trailer. "Will as soon as I'm done."

"You're done now. That chapter who fucked with your tattoo shop? They're here."

"Here, as in on the grounds?" I pointed to the county parkland surrounding us.

"Here, as in, holed up in a shack they are using to cook shit five miles south of here."

"Meth?"

Mike nodded, still scanning the area. His paranoia spooked me. I took a quick look-see past his six, but nothing was out of place.

"Pot, pharmaceuticals, you name it. I got a guy on the inside who let me know the location, so I watched it. They've been coming and going out of there for almost two weeks now."

"Shit. You could have told me sooner." But then again, I hadn't checked in with him until last night because I needed to know if someone could take Ant in. I was done looking behind me and needed to move on faster than I could with Ant declining like he was. Betty Jo would bitch, but eventually, see my point. I hoped.

"It gets worse."

I rolled my eyes because I really didn't want to get sucked into Mike's games. I could imagine how it was worse and let those thoughts form out loud. "Lemme guess, some of it's ours."

He stopped his scanning to skewer me with his stare. "How'd you know?"

Shit, it was easy. "It's a typical setup. You stuff drugs into the parts, ship 'em like freight, but the shipment got nicked, and then you showed up here. It wasn't the parts you were looking for. It was the drugs inside, wasn't it?"

One of the main reasons I got out when Ant closed up shop was because of this kind of stupidity. The bike riding part was easy. Protecting hundreds of thousands worth of drugs wasn't. People like Big Mike and I were killers thanks to the ever-rolling movement of this or that substance from state to state or country to country. There was always some asshole wanting a slice of the business, no matter how fiercely you protected your territory.

"You are too damn smart for your own good. But also fucking stupid. I came here to tell you that, you know?"

"Done told me. You can leave now." I was sick of taking others' shit. Betty Jo was right. Getting a steady diet of compliments was a million times better than smoke up the ass.

"Are you serious about quitting the club?"

"Told you I was."

He soaked that in for a moment. Then gestured at the mountains.

"The Wicked Legion already think you're dead. You don't need to make the job of killing you again easier."

Maybe I didn't want to be dead. Maybe I wanted a life of festivals and fairs and Betty Jo at my side. Hiding wasn't going to get me that. "Did you get a hold of Tipton?" Old Hoss ran the support chapter in Maryland. He owed Mike and I big time.

"Caught his son. He says the cabin is ready if you need it."

Good. Hopefully, the kid's old man hadn't leaked any of our secrets to him.

"That's a good spot for ya. I'll sleep better at night knowing you're there watching over things," Mike hinted.

We'd buried three sets of bones on the property. They weren't the only skeletons in Mike and mine's closets, but they were the ones most closely connected to us. "Maybe burn them when you get a chance, hey?"

"I'll do that." I kept an eye on the park. That loud boat puttered past again, spewing water and smelling like the fuel it leaked.

Out of habit, I reached into my pocket and pulled out my knife. I flipped it open and shut as I waited. Can't say what I was waiting for, but the world was holding its breath for some reason.

Flick, click, snap, click, flick. Over and over.

"You hear that?" A familiar rumble of motorcycles echoed off the hills. The sound came from the highway, so there was nothing out of place about it. But the noise put me on edge.

"I hear it. I best help you pack up, get you moving quicker."

"Thanks, brother."

I bent down to pick up the pile of billets at my feet.

A fast-moving object slapped my hood and pinged off the fence behind me.

Mike dropped to one knee and whipped his pistol out. He fired at someone running away.

I hit his arm because I didn't know if the person was friend or foe. Worse still, we were in a public park. Exchanging gunfire was bound to get noticed quickly.

"What the fuck? You made me miss," Big Mike hissed.

"Get the fuck out of here. Go."

"They were aiming for you." Mike tugged on my hood and stuck a finger through the hole.

Seeing it wiggle there slammed things home. "They found us." Or he led them here.

"Get Ant. I'll bring the truck around."

"Fuck. Betty Jo," I cursed, realizing that Mike did not know she was with us.

"Oh, you have got to be shitting me! You really have a death wish, don't you?" He caught on fast.

I didn't have time to answer Mike. I lit off across the grounds to the RV.

But when I got there, it was empty. Okay. Not completely empty.

Ant was on the floor, blood poured from stab wounds. He wheezed and reached for me when I entered. I went to my knees; the blood that soaked into my jeans was warm.

"Don't die on me." I tried to put pressure on the wounds, but there were too many to cover.

"They got her." He gripped my shirt, leaving a stain of blood there.

"Betty Jo?"

Ant's eyes went closed as if to say yes. "Tried to kill him, missed. Sorry, son." He pantomimed throwing a knife, but his motion flopped to the floor. The grip of his other hand loosened, and I caught his arm before it, too, landed.

"Ant," I begged him to hold on, but it was too late. He was gone. The lines of pain relaxed as his will fled, and he breathed his last.

I hung my head. Paralyzed by grief. The trailer rocked as someone came up the stairs.

It wasn't Mike because the guy was trying to be quiet and failed.

"You *are* alive. I told Roger you were."

Betty Jo's cousin stood at the door, a bloody knife in hand. I made the connection to the stuff I was drowning in. "Did you kill Ant?"

The smile on Theo's face was macabre. "Yeah. He was a fucking Destroyer. I killed a Destroyer," he practically crowed.

Flick, snap, click. Then *slice, slice, stab.* Theo fell backward to the dirt at the bottom of the steps with me on top of him. I cut his throat last. His fingers clutched at the air. Hot blood poured out of his thigh and his gut. The stuff at his neck barely had pressure to pump out and pulsed sluggishly into the grass.

"A fucking Destroyer killed you," I whispered into his ear as I watched the light drain from his eyes.

Big Mike rolled up with his truck. "Get in."

I looked around. A siren sounded in the distance. "Shit." I glanced at Theo in the dirt, then back to the camper. "Ant's in there."

"Get him."

"He's dead."

Mike's shoulders slumped. He shut off the engine and crawled out of the cab. He did a scan of the area and came to a decision. "Okay. Stuff the body in there and take off. I'll fix the dirt and keep my eyes and ears open here. Drive to the farthest campsite you can get to up on that ridge. I'll meet you there. Don't fucking break any speed limits, and don't get caught."

"They got Betty Jo."

"And you'll not be able to get her back if you're in jail."

He had a damn good point. I hefted up Theo's body and tossed him next to Ant's. Then took one of the clean towels Betty Jo insisted I buy and wiped down the outside. I tossed it onto the seat next to me. "Make it fast, and don't let them detain you," I told Mike.

Over half an hour later, Mike joined me on the ridge. I'd watched the park. A police cruiser stopped briefly to investigate the gunshots and left empty-handed. My guess was that no one saw anything, just heard the noises, and were spooked into calling 911. My hands shook as I cleaned the blood off my skin. Some of it caked under my fingernails and in the cracks. I dug at it, trying my damnedest to get rid of it.

"Spoke with one of those festival guys. No one knows what happened. They already think it was that damn boat misfiring."

"That's good." My voice was hoarse.

He noticed my shaking hands. "You getting soft on me?"

I clenched my fingers into fists. Then shook them out. "Do you think they took Betty Jo to that house you mentioned?"

"Probably."

"Let's go."

He put a hand on my chest. "Hold up. Think for a minute. That's where they are going to expect you to go. You might wanna take a minute to ask yourself if she's worth it."

I scowled at him. Then I pointed at the trailer and kept my voice as quiet as I could. "I got two dead bodies in there. One with damn incriminating wounds that match no less than three other DBs around this fucking country. I'm willing to let that sit out here in the middle of fucking nowhere like a goddamned neon sign because, yeah, she's worth it. Even if I killed her cousin." That's what was bothering me most.

Dumbass that he was, Big Mike started laughing.

I slumped down and planted my butt on the steps. *Asshole.*

Big Mike squeezed my shoulders and got down to my level to look me in the eye. "You did what you had to. I found a bloody knife. Did he catch you anywhere?"

"The blood is Ant's."

"Really?" Big Mike shoved past me and stepped into the RV.

A second later, he hopped over me and landed in the dirt.

"Christ." His hand covered his heart.

"Bastard bragged about it before I sliced him up." I spit into the dirt between my feet, trying to do anything but think. But try as I might, the pain slammed home. "He's gone. Ant's gone."

All those days I thought I had left? Robbed. Taken from me by my enemy. But also, he was Betty Jo's blood. How would I reconcile that? I loved her. But that piece of her, the blood she came from, how could I love that? Moreover, how would she ever love me now that I'd taken my vengeance out on her cousin?

Those dreams I had of traveling the country with Betty Jo at my side? They were gone. Spilled out like rivers into the California dust. My knife did that.

My anger did that.

That's why my hands shook.

It wasn't just losing Ant that ripped me apart. It was losing the dream.

There would be no peaceful solution now. Never. Not until Ant's death was avenged on every Wicked Legion patch-holder this side of the Rockies.

Mike pulled me up and wrapped me in his arms. "Gotcha, brother. I gotcha." He slapped me on the back and squeezed tighter. I wished like hell it was Betty Jo here hugging me instead. But it meant a lot for my oldest brother to be here helping me share the grief.

His phone rang, breaking us apart.

He looked at the caller and scowled. "Keep quiet. It's my contact."

Instantly, hatred bubbled up like a wellhead inside me. The same urge to kill that led my hand when I sliced Theo up made my fingers itch. Whoever was on that phone would die, even if they were our ally. Hell, the thought that Mike had been courting one of Ant's murderers made me hate him.

It took every ounce of patience I had to keep quiet. There was a divide between us. At that moment, I knew we couldn't go back to a few seconds ago. Mike was no more my brother than any stranger. I wasn't thinking right. Not at all. But without Ant, without Betty Jo, my life didn't matter. Loyalties would be bought with blood. And anyone standing in my way would go down, Destroyer or enemy.

Mike spoke not more than six words and did a lot of listening before he hung up and said, "He took her to a motel. Says we need to hurry."

"Who took her?"

"Bones."

Flick. Click.

"Easy, Fin. He's helping us. Says he's trying to keep her safe so we can come get her."

"He's how you knew I was following her, right?"

Mike looked away. "Couldn't stick a prospect on it."

I laughed once bitterly. "So, you stuck the goddamn enemy on it. Christ."

"You were right. He's tired of being in Roger's shadow. Wants us to kill his president so he can take over."

Fuck. "Take over what?" There wasn't going to be anything left.

The look Mike gave me held suspicion. "What are you planning, Fin?"

I locked eyes with him. "I'm going to kill every one of them."

"Over a girl?"

"Over Ant."

He looked away and licked his lips. "Yeah." But he wasn't ready to agree to my plan yet. "We can't kill all of them."

"Watch me."

"Fuck. I know what you're capable of, but…"

"Watch me," I repeated. As in, watch over me. Be a good brother. *Have my back for fucking once.* All my life I'd done anything he'd asked of me. Anything the club asked. What I wasn't saying but begging for was right there. *Please, Mike, be my family. Be loyal.*

Finally, he nodded. "We're doing this together. Understand?"

Hell yes.

We could take his truck and make better time, but we also needed to move the RV. A hotel parking lot was good camouflage.

"I'll follow you," I said.

CHAPTER 19

Bones was on the phone with Roger, selling me out. It was his second call.
The first had been Big Mike, telling him where to come get me.
He said the same thing to Roger. Whatever his game was, it was rotten to
the core.

We were holed up in an abandoned shit-hole motel slammed between
the wrong side of town and the worst side of town. The mattress smelled like
moldy vomit. I didn't dare move for fear I might sit in something... *organic*.
The thought made me queasy.

"No, I can't get a hold of Bear. I told the bastard to take care of the
other one but not get caught. Betcha he got caught," he yammered on.

Or killed. Roger was on his way. And he was mad as hell and getting
angrier since Theo found me with Ant and Bones.

There was a ton of stuff Fin and I got wrong.

We'd thought Ant was buying from someone at the festival. Never in our
wildest dreams did we suspect what was really going on.

Come to find out, Ant was buying his drugs from the Wicked Legion.
Bones, specifically. At some point after his last chemo treatment, Bones
caught him trying to buy pot from a street dealer. In exchange for a direct
connection to the Wicked Legion's drug supply, Bones had been pumping
him for information and a connection to the Destroyers.

If there was a top prize for stupidity, I don't know who would win it today. Theo for following Bones on a drug drop. Ant for buying drugs from the enemy. Or me, for waltzing into the middle of a really fucked up situation and getting dragged out of it by my hair.

The scene washed over me again. It felt like the hundredth time I relived seeing Ant killed.

Bones walked in on me putting the dishes away.

"Holy shit-damn. Roger has been looking all over for you."

I dropped the plate in my hand. It bounced on the floor and hit me in the shin. "What in the hell are you doing here?"

Then Ant came out of the back wearing only his pajama bottoms.

"Hey, Bones. Got my shit?" He limped past me and sat down in the booth, pulling out his shake box.

I saw red. "You've been buying drugs from the Wicked Legion?"

"How long have you been here?" Bones asked over my question.

"Fuck you."

"Not with a ten-foot dick. Bitch."

That *word*. I picked up the closet cup and whipped it at his head. Of course, I missed. Even if I had hit the target, that stupid solo plastic wouldn't have done any damage. But my nails sure could.

"Hey now, just give me the shit." Ant stood up and tried to tug Bones and me apart.

Bones elbowed him backward onto the table. The top flipped off, and Ant hit the floor. I kicked Bones in the leg and went to help Ant.

Then things got worse.

Theo walked in, cell phone to one ear. "Yeah, Prez, I followed him to an old trailer in the park. I think he's... Oh shit, Betty Jo, what the fuck?"

Which meant Roger knew I was there.

Ant grabbed the knife Fin brought back from the smithy last night and took aim at Theo.

Instinctively, I tried to stop him and fouled his throw.

The blade bounced against the door and clattered to the floor of the RV. Ant rolled onto his stomach and stretched to grab it, and Theo saw the Destroyers tattoo on his back.

"Goddamn it. He's a Destroyer!" Theo jumped on top of Ant, crushing him with his weight. He pulled out his own knife and stabbed Ant right in the middle of the tattoo. Then pulled it out and stabbed him in the shoulder.

I screamed.

Bones grabbed me from behind, covering my mouth. I bit his hand, and he shoved me hard.

I fell into the cabinet edge, and Bones got a hold of my hair.

As he dragged me out of the RV, Theo rolled Ant over and stabbed him once more, right in the chest. He turned his head and looked me straight in the eye. "Got him."

The fight went out of me as I blubbered for him to stop. But it was too late. I turned to Bones.

"Please let me help him. Please!"

Bones didn't listen. No one listened to me.

My cousin slapped me. "Shut your fucking big mouth, Betty Jo."

But I couldn't.

"Fin is going to kill you."

Bones shoved me into a nondescript sedan. And I realized my mistake. Theo was right; I had a big fucking mouth. Stupid nomination number two.

"Fin, huh?" Theo narrowed his eyes at me before turning to Bones. "He didn't die like we thought."

"Get him," Bones ordered.

"You think she's been fucking him?" Theo made a face.

"Don't care. He's going to be dead, right?"

"Damn straight." Theo glared at me and pointed to the tears on my face. "That's what you get for sleeping with the enemy. You and your dad, both fucking traitors. I hope Roger kills you, too."

That son of a bitch. He knew all along how my father died. Any love I had for him shriveled up. I hated him. I hated all of them. As Bones pulled away, Theo pulled his gun and stalked off to kill Fin.
I cried halfway to the motel before realizing I had the knife Ant tossed at Theo tucked between the folds of my nightgown. I don't know when I scooped it up. Maybe while Theo was stabbing Ant, or maybe when Bones tossed me into the counter. Either way, I had a chance.

Cue entry number three on my part for the stupid award. I tried to threaten Bones with the knife.

In two seconds, he had it out of my hands and tucked into a boot.

Then he cold-cocked me.

I woke up as he dragged me into the motel room. The rag he put in my mouth tasted like sweat and dirt.

The motel smelled worse. I sat on the bed, trying not to gag, and waited for Bones to get distracted. But he watched me like a hawk.

"Told you, I've been looking for her ever since her car was sold."

That's how they tracked me here. Fin took me two towns over to buy a shitty truck. Then we went to another town and sold my car. I paid him what I got from the trade-in, but we hadn't signed any paperwork. Obviously, the paperwork for my car was filed. I should have just abandoned it.

Outside the window was Bones' bike. The sedan was parked next to it. The keys for both were hooked on Bones' belt. There was no way I could get the keys off him by force.

I needed another way. There were no weapons in the room heavy enough to knock Bones out except the TV. And it was bolted to the wall. Charming.

Bones put away his phone and grabbed my face.

"Your cousin fucked things up for me." Since I had a nasty rag in my mouth, I didn't have to answer. Instead, I twisted out of his grip and turned to face the window. There I sat, holding onto any dignity I had left.

Not that there was much to be had.

My nightgown was torn down the front, and it had blood splatter on the hem. I had no weapons, not even words.

"I was getting good intel from that Destroyer so he could feed his habit."

Maybe I should pay attention to this. If I survived, I'd tell Fin. He could tell whomever he had to that Ant had sold them out.

"He even told me where to hit that shipment of parts."

The ones at my father's shop and at the swap meet. I glared at Bones. He knew all along where those parts came from and let my father take the blame.

Oh.

The pieces fell together. Roger killed my father for being a snitch. But Bones was a bigger one. *Asshole.*

A bike rumbled up to the curb left of where Bones' bike was parked. Roger got off and hung his helmet. He gave his hair a toss before studying the parking lot like he owned the entire world. I used to think that was sexy. Now it hit my gut like acid. I slept with that son of a bitch.

The smell from the gag curdled in my nose and, coupled with understanding what lay below Roger's facade of good looks, made my stomach churn.

"Shut up, Betty Jo. You might just survive." Bones opened the door and ushered Roger in with a slap on the back and a smile.

"Any word from Theo yet?" Roger asked.

"None."

"Fucker better not have gotten caught." Roger tilted his head and took in my ripped nightgown, the bruises from where Bones hit me, the scraped knees, the gag, and my icy glare. "You have been a lot of trouble lately, Betty Jo."

His eyes lingered on my tits.

"Take the gag out. I want answers," he demanded.

Bones did as ordered and stepped aside like a good little soldier. I knew better.

Roger stepped between my legs. "First things first, were you with that asshole Destroyer?"

"Ant needed help."

His slap knocked me over. Roger's voice went cold and low. "Not that Destroyer. The other one."

He meant Fin. I wasn't going to give that up if I could help it. But my cheek stung, and my jaw wouldn't hold up to another blow like that one. "There's over eight-hundred Destroyers in the U.S. Be a bit more specific."

Roger bent down on one knee. His hands slid up my legs, not stopping until my underwear was exposed. He paused there and looked me in the eye.

I barely dared to breathe.

"The one you are fucking." His voice was cold and flat. The same inflection he used when giving the order to kill someone.

Before I could answer, his thumbs dug into the tender hollow near my femoral arteries. The nerve clusters there shot pain through my system from my toenails to my scalp. I screamed.

He dug in harder. I tried to get away from him, but he grabbed my crotch.

It didn't hurt, but it was a threat that made me freeze.

"You fucked him, didn't you?" Bones made a noise that drew Roger's attention. "What?"

"Should I watch for Theo?" The displeasure on his face was clear.

Roger stood up. He made a show of looking out the window. "Don't see him yet, so no."

There wasn't time for Bones to hide the flash of disgust that slid across his face.

"What's that face for?" Roger stalked him like a cat.

"Nothing."

"No, I think it's something. Either you don't wanna watch me fuck my old lady, or you are angry it ain't your turn. Which is it?"

"I am not your old lady."

"Shut up, *bitch*!" Roger whirled around, both fists in motion. I cowered like a dog, taking blow after blow. My arms were bruised, my face battered, and Roger was only getting started.

He stepped away and kicked me in the ribcage. Then once more, in a blow that caught my hip.

"You bitch. You whore. It was probably you all along who gave those Destroyer fucks our secrets. You sold us out. Slut. Fat cow. Bet you fucked them both because you're so desperate to get laid."

Another kick landed and knocked the wind out of me. I kept curled to avoid as much damage as possible. But the tirade of insults flowed into my soul.

"You were once so pretty. Now you're a cheap cunt who got her father killed because you couldn't keep your legs and lips shut."

He was so wrong.

I uncurled to fight back, but I wasn't the only one in the room with an agenda.

Bones caught Roger around the neck. The blade he'd taken from me in the car held at Roger's throat. "It didn't have to be this way. But I'm sick of waiting for my turn."

Roger twisted, somehow avoiding getting his throat slit and trapping Bones' hand with the knife.

"The traitor reveals himself," Roger said coldly.

Bones cursed.

"What was it? Money? Did they offer you a patch? Power? Or her?" Roger spit at me but missed.

I crawled up to balance on a knee and catch my breath. Blood dripped onto the nasty carpet and disappeared into the other stains there.

"King, I swear I'm loyal. I swear."

"Bullshit. You are a traitor. Wanna know how I know?"

"You don't know shit." Bones put more weight into their struggle for control of the knife.

Roger laughed. "Tell him, Betty Jo. Tell him how I knew. You saw it, didn't you?"

I had. Even though I didn't hear who he called first, I knew how Bones had been bought.

"Saddlebags," I wheezed. Bones' bike sat in the sun with my custom bags tied to the back.

Roger punched Bones in the stomach and twisted his grip hard to dislodge the knife. It fell to the carpet and stuck there, stabbing the floor at an angle.

Then, he drew his gun and shot Bones through the temple. For the second time that morning, I was splattered with gore.

What was left of his vice president tumbled to the floor with a thud. Blood leaked out of the fatal wound. The carpet turned almost black where it soaked in.

Roger holstered his gun and laughed manically. "You noticed them, didn't you? Of course you did." He slapped his leg, tickled pink with his amusement.

I moved closer to the bed, hoping my ex-husband's mercurial temper was finally sated. Just in case, I clutched Ant's knife close to my side.

It took a full minute for Roger to sober up. When he did, I didn't like the glint in his eye. "Get on the bed."

Shit.

I crept stiffly to keep the pain from overpowering my senses. "Don't hit me again. Please?"

He unbuckled his belt. "I love it when you beg. Remember the good old days?" He snapped the leather together with a "crack."

Not fondly. I was off the floor, but not fully on the bed. He'd have to get close now. I bit my lip, remembering how easily Bones had disarmed me. But losing the knife the first time reminded me of what Ant said about the blacksmith knife in my hand. It was shaped like a shepherd's crook, being hammered from a strip of metal and bent around in a twisty "U" to form the handle. You could tie a cord in the oblong loop there or slip your fingers inside so it wouldn't get knocked free. I did that now. The little three-inch blade was shorter than the width of my hand. The surface was black except where the edge was honed to almost razor sharpness.

"I said, get on the bed." Roger approached and grabbed my legs to position me.

With both of his hands full, it was easy to stab him in the groin. Twice.

Then I slashed at his stomach and his arms as he tried to stop the blood.

He fell to his knees, and I grabbed his hair, pulling his head back to expose his neck.

"You're a real bitch, Betty Jo," he wheezed.

"Yes. I am."

The skin of his neck was much thinner than other parts. Ant's knife slipped through it like cutting air. Emboldened by that, I sliced again. The heel of the blade caught on something gristly, so I yanked it free and stabbed harder, hacking away at his neck with intentions of sawing his head clean off.

I didn't get that far. But I damn sure tried.

CHAPTER 20

Before we approached the motel, Mike tugged me to the side. "I didn't know you had Betty Jo."

"Would it have changed anything?"

"Hell, yes. I'd have gotten her out. You know that, brother."

I didn't know how I could trust him. He admitted to getting information from Bones. "Maybe, maybe not." I started moving again.

He stopped me with a hand on the shoulder. "We got loyalty, Fin. It goes way back. That's how you know what I'm saying is true. We're Destroyers. We're assholes, but loyal assholes, got it?"

Maybe if I agreed, we'd get moving faster. "Are you done?"

"Yeah, guess so."

He went in first, crashing through the door like it was paper.

The scene was brutal.

Betty Jo huddled in the corner behind the bed. Whether or not she knew it, she whimpered. My heart bled for her. Her eyes were red and held a glaze of madness. As much as I wanted to rush over and hold her, get her through whatever nightmare she was trapped by, I held back. The blade in her hand wasn't coming free any time soon. Mike noticed both my hesitation and her state and followed my lead. I hoped she'd snap out of it while we pieced together the scene. Otherwise, things might get dicier than they already were.

From the looks of things, Roger had killed Bones. And Betty Jo had butchered Roger. For a three-inch blade, it did a lot of damage. Ant made excellent weapons. That memory carried a lot of guilt and grief. I should have been there.

Of course, if I had been in that trailer, I'd likely be dead right now. And no one would have been able to tip Big Mike off. Where would that have left Betty Jo?

Damn it. She'd be dead, or worse.

Enough what-ifs. I had to come to grips with reality.

And while we were doing that, figure out a way to tell her about her cousin. *Jesus.* Would she want me after finding out that I'd killed the only family she had left? Maybe that's why it was easier to stay away from her than to comfort her. And if that wasn't an asshole thing to do, I don't know what was.

"I'll scope out the building. Maybe we can torch the whole thing." Mike's words broke me out of my trance.

"What is it with you and fire?" I asked.

"You're one to talk," he pointed out.

Well, there was truth to his point. But generally, it was fire I could control. Mike's suggestion wasn't a bad idea. Betty Jo's blood was here, too. Fire would foul any evidence.

A lot of her blood was here. That made me angry. If I could kill Roger all over again, I'd make him pay. While my cuts might be more meticulous than Betty Jo's, I'd have butchered the motherfucker, too.

I started expanding on Mike's plans. "You're going to need at least three gallons of gas, and the bodies still won't burn completely. God help us if the fire department or police get here before it catches."

"They'll blame it on the war."

Mike's voice faded into the background. My brain froze. All I could see was my girl, panicked, in pain, and wary. In the few directions I'd spoken, she'd looked up and seen me. The real me.

"Fin?" Her voice bled fear.

I closed my eyes, knowing what was going to happen next would hurt. "Mike, take her outside."

"No. I gotta siphon off some gas from that car out there. She's your old lady. Talk to her."

"I ain't his old lady. Yet." Betty Jo stood up and wobbled a bit. She brushed the knife blade clean on what was left of her nightgown. Not that it got spotless, with all the blood soaking the fabric.

"You're right. You ain't. Now get outside with Mike while I stage this shit."

"Finnigan Curty, look at me."

Very cautiously, I did.

Her eyes met mine. They were hard.

I swallowed, wondering if she knew I'd killed her cousin. Was the deed etched onto my face?

Then, in a blink, whatever passed between us was stuffed away.

"I'm a mess." She tugged the nightgown away from her skin. It stuck in places, and she made a face. "Tell me the RV is here."

I cleared my throat. "You can't go in there."

Her perfectly arched brow shot higher. "Excuse me?"

"I don't want you to go in there until..." *Aw fuck.* Until I moved her cousin's body out, at least.

"Ant's still in there, isn't he?"

The words, if I had any, got stuck in my mouth.

"I'm sorry, Fin."

"So am I." I was talking about Theo. But she didn't know that.

"Get me something to wear. I'll take a shower in here and—" Her words cut off as she looked inside the bathroom. "Ugh. On second thought, I'll take my chances in the RV."

I cleared my throat. "You can't."

"Fin? Are you feeling okay?"

"I killed Theo."

Big Mike took that moment to butt his ugly ass into our conversation. "Self-defense, not murder."

"Stay out of this," I warned.

"Can't have you going around and sabotaging a good lay just because your conscience decided to wake up."

"You wanna help?" Betty Jo asked.

"Um... huh?" Even Big Mike knew a loaded question when he heard it.

"Go in that RV, find me a decent set of clothes, and grab the baby wipes from the back cabinet. It's off to the left as you go into what supposedly is a bedroom. Third shelf. You can't miss the stack of boxes. They're bright blue." She shooed her hands at Mike. "Get!"

Surprisingly, Mike obeyed.

"As for you,"

"Said I'm sorry. Not going to make any excuses. He killed Ant."

"I know. I saw him do it."

Jesus.

I held my hands out. But she was covered in drying blood, and there was just something damn awkward about offering to hug someone in that state.

"Don't just stand there. Go help Mike move Theo. Torching this place is probably the end it deserves." Under her breath, she mumbled, "If it will even burn under all this mold."

For that, she got a slap on the ass and a peck on the ear. That part of her body was fairly clean and unmarked. I paused a moment to take in the red marks and bruises. "You sound okay, but are you?"

"I'll be okay."

"Like I said, you sound okay, but are you sure?"

"Yes." She sounded so certain. I wish I could have had that same confidence.

Two weeks later, the Henderson chapter hosted Ant's funeral ride. Don't ask me how they got everything arranged. Betty Jo and I took Mike's truck across the border while he cleaned up the RV and transported Ant's body. The coroner on their payroll signed off on his death as cancer-related heart failure. I bet that cost a bundle.

The pack of bikes stretched for miles. The spot for family was left empty. Mike thought it best we let my legend die along with the Wicked Legion we torched.

I masked up and rode along, safely ensconced in the pack. There was more than one nomad paying respects. But Ant's urn was strapped under my coat. The hearse held an empty coffin. I should take his ashes back to Minnesota. Or maybe I'd seed a new forge with them. I hadn't planned that far ahead yet. Hell, I had no plans at all except to get through the funeral.

Betty Jo, sheathed in black from head to toe, joined me at the fringes of the group while bikers from all over paid respects. The pack of bikes revved loud. Gardnerville's road captain led the send-off. Three times we redlined our engines. The roar of hundreds of bikes echoed against the mountains and called back to us like ghosts.

The tail-gunner from our old chapter in Minnesota answered those echoes with a single, long roaring wail of a throaty thousand CCs screaming its heart out for a brother.

I reached over to hold Betty Jo's hand. She leaned on my shoulder, tears visible under the veil she wore. The silence broke when Big Mike got off his bike and began walking down the line of bikes. The first fifty riders in the procession got commemorative patches. I was the last one graced with the black fabric. Stitched into the little rectangle were three things. "Ant."

The years he rode with us, and on the final line, an abbreviation meaning, "Gone, but not forgotten." I tucked it away to sew on later.

With that, the crowd thinned. There was a party back at the clubhouse, but I wasn't going to attend.

Instead, I was behind the wheel of Big Mike's truck on our way back into Wicked Legion territory with Betty Jo.

"Take me back," she'd said. So I was. Silence wrapped around us, helped by Ant's urn strapped into the seat between us.

"Turn left here." She pointed out the direction.

The road dead-ended at a city cemetery. I parked the truck, and Betty Jo didn't wait for me to open her door. She slammed the door hard behind her.

I debated whether I should try to catch up to her or sit it out. But the truck didn't have AC, so the latter choice was a matter of discomfort. I threw my coat over Ant's urn and followed.

She stood between two gravestones, hands on her hips.

As I walked up, she pointed to a larger stone just a few feet away. "Grandpa. Just beyond that stone is one of my uncles."

I looked at the closest stone. Engraved on the face was her father's name, and under it, his nickname, "Wrench." Below those lines were the typical dates of birth and death. Then an inscription, "Loving Father, Loving Brother." On the line under it were four tiny letters. "GBNF," just like Ant's patch. I knew Betty Jo ordered the inscription. We weren't that much different, her and I. Both of us adhering to tradition despite what we'd endured.

Theo's grave was not as fancy. Just his name and the dates. I don't know who arranged that one. It hadn't been Betty Jo.

The papers speculated Theo's death was a drug deal gone wrong. Cops busted the lab on the same day, catching the rest of the Wicked Legion red-handed. One whole chapter removed in a single moment. Big Mike was soaking up the praise for that one. Someone had to, because I was supposedly dead and aimed to remain that way.

"What you going to do next?" I asked.

"I'm going to go home."

Her words hit me like a sledgehammer. I didn't say a word in argument. Instead, I quietly walked away to let her have her moment with her family. They didn't need Theo's murderer hanging out with the only surviving member left.

Hot or not, I waited with the truck so I could drive her back to the house.

When parked out front, I tried to muster the courage to apologize once more. Hell, a hundred times more. But the words got stuck.

Betty Jo broke the silence with a "huff."

"I'll be right back."

The door slammed shut, rocking the truck. I watched her sashay to the front door, bend over, and pull a key out from a hidden hole. Then she disappeared inside.

Be right back?

Maybe she needed me to take her back to retrieve that old truck? I supposed that made sense. I hadn't been thinking right since I found Ant lying in his own blood.

Betty Jo jumped back inside, a plastic bin in her hands and a shotgun under one arm.

"What's that?" I said, pointing at the bin. On closer inspection, it was packed with a couple of blankets.

"It's a blanket bin."

"I can see that. Why do you need a bunch of blankets?"

"Because the papers for the house, Pa's bank records, and copies of the deed to the garage are in it. I need to go to the bank."

That made sense, I guess. Why she needed the whole damn bin was confusing, though.

I put the truck in gear and drove her to the bank. Outside, I handed her the truck keys. "I'll call Mike and catch a ride back."

"Why?"

"You're going to need the truck."

"Why?"

I stared at her. "To get around until someone drives your truck here."

When she didn't answer, I tried to clear up the confusion. "I know we didn't talk about it, and I understand if you want nothing to do with me because of… well, things. Theo, specifically. But I—Hell. There's nothing for me here."

"Fin, shut up."

My jaw snapped shut, and my head reared back. "Did you just—"

"I'm going with you. I just had to say goodbye and take care of this shit." She lifted the box in her hands. "Once I close out Pa's accounts, we're out of here and kissing California good-fucking-riddance."

She'd rendered me speechless once again. *Damn.*

"Stay right here until I'm out. Understand? Else I'm using Pa's shotgun to plug a few holes in your hide. We're going to Maryland. But I'll be damned if I'm living in a little shack of a cabin forever. I'm hoping the sale of the shop and the house will get us a farm. Maybe one with a big enough barn you can set up your forge."

I tried one last time to make her see reason. All that talk we did before Ant died didn't mean anything anymore. She had her life back. The Wicked Legion were locked up or dead. She had options. I didn't. "You don't *have* to go with me."

"The hell I don't. Like you said, there's nothing for me here, either. Now quit standing there with your mouth hanging open and find some shade. Better yet, go over to that restaurant and get us some takeout. We're going to need food and fuel for the road."

Man, I was a lucky son of a bitch. A beautiful, confident woman was ordering me around. I kind of liked it. What I liked more was that she wanted to be with me. Me. Huh.

It took the better part of the day just to get back to Nevada.

There we holed up in a family hotel for a day or five while Mike got the RV deep cleaned and my trailer hauled to Maryland.

Betty Jo came out of the shower with her hair wrapped up in a towel. The other towel was tucked together just above her boobs. The edges gaped open and flashed the mesmerizingly soft curves of her thigh.

"Come here." I tapped the bed.

"I'm all wet."

"I'll make you wetter." Remembering the taste of her, I licked my lips. I couldn't wait to get between her thighs again.

"You are incorrigible."

"That means horny, right?"

She smiled, humoring me. I knew damn well what she meant, but played stupid anyway. It was our little way of showing affection. Giving each other shit.

I tugged on the towel, pulling it free. "Whoops. Now you're naked."

She climbed on top, straddling me. Her reflection looked good in the hotel mirror opposite us, except for one thing. I put my hands over that damn property stamp. "Before we get on the road, I'm gonna get you into the local shop. See if they'll let me use their kit and get your tattoo finished."

Betty Jo glanced behind her and saw what I saw in the mirror. "Christ. Can we go now?"

"Nope."

"Why not?"

I grinned. "Lift up and turn around." I directed her onto her hands and knees. Then I put my hand right over that stupid mark. With the other, I held my dick and ran the head up and down her exposed pussy. "Going to come all over it tonight. Tomorrow, it will be my mark on you. Understood?"

She twisted around to glare at me. "You gonna yap about it, or do it?"

Well, shit. She had a point. I stopped talking and started doing. She wasn't lying, she was wet. There. I slipped inside and slowly worked all the way in. I grabbed her hips so she wouldn't move.

"Mine."

I slid out halfway, admiring the glistening residue on my shaft. Then slid back in as slow as I could possibly go.

She squirmed under my hands. "Harder, please?"

"In a minute." On the next thrust inside, I urged her to finger herself. I wasn't going to last long enough or hold on to my shit if I had to wait.

The next four strokes came faster. Then I lost my self-control. Her knuckles brushed my dick, and I had to take her hard.

She moaned, "That's it. Hammer hard."

Don't have to tell me more than twice. Our bodies slapped each time I drove deep. Betty Jo braced both hands on the bed and pushed back on me as much as I surged forward. I grabbed her, tilting us forward and grinding her deep into the mattress. My harsh words begged her to come.

She brushed my dick again as she furiously rubbed her clit. I pounded away, hitting her deep. She cried out.

The sound stretched as she found the right spot and held her body taunt to make it last.

Then she came with a rush of pulsing wet flutters around my dick. I was balls deep and holding on for dear life, waiting until she was done and pushing hard.

Her body relaxed. As she fell apart, I pumped hard to chase my own high. It came on cue. But damn, it was tough to pull out.

The sight of my semen on her back, though? Worth it. Someday I'd come on my ink there. But for that moment? Ha. One last 'fuck you' to Roger and his shit. I smeared the fluid around, painting it into her skin, drawing a shark with my fingertip in the mess.

"That tickles. What are you doing?"

"Finger painting."

"You're like a damn kid."

I chuckled.

"I'm going to have to take another shower."

"I got it." I took the discarded towel and wiped away the bulk of the mess. Then went to the bathroom to get a damp cloth to do the job right.

Later, when the night was quiet and deep, we talked about everything. Ant, her Pa, the Wicked Legion, even my parents. Some of it wasn't good. Other parts were funny as hell.

"Promise me something, Fin?"

"Anything." I meant it.

"Don't ever call me a bitch."

I looked at her with all the questions written on my face.

"Just please, don't."

"You aren't a bitch. Any fool would know that."

She grunted as if to say I was wrong.

I tugged her in tight. "You are beautiful. Courageous. Kind. Loving. Sweet. Spicy. Salty, hot as fuck, but not a bitch. Whoever said that was an idiot."

"Yeah, they were."

Something in her tone clued me in on the fact she was thinking about her family or the Wicked Legion.

"We're putting those days behind us."

She smiled and met my eyes. Her quiet, "Thank you," was all I needed. We were going into the unknown. But at least we were going together.

CHAPTER 21

One year later.

Welp, the bloom was off the rose. The single-bedroom cabin we called home was too damn small, and there was nothing that would help make it bigger short of dynamite and a bulldozer. However, without it, my brand-new pile of faun suede would get ruined in the infernal rainstorms that boomed non-stop from Memorial Day to the Fourth of July.

But I had an answer.

And that answer involved a quick road trip. Well, it was more complicated than that. With all the finagling out of the way, I got Fin to fire up the old pickup and gave him directions to a small community on the outskirts of Hagerstown, Maryland.

The subdivision held little two- and three-bedroom ranch homes. Each one was almost a cardboard cutout of the house next door. Near the end, the road took an abrupt turn off into the fields beyond.

"Turn left."

"The road turns right."

"Our stop is on the left. That driveway."

Fin almost overshot my directions, and I had the overwhelming urge to yell at him, but kept my tone as sweet as honey mead because I needed him in a good mood for what came next. I'd pinned too many hopes on this place. It fell into that sweet spot of just the right amount of land to justify barns, but none of the hassle of actual farming. *Fuck that shit.* The price was right, too. No one wanted to buy a farm they couldn't use. Except us—if Fin agreed with my choice. This was the last hurdle. If it failed, bulldozer time.

The truck rocked as it hit a pothole washed into the gravel. Peeling paint exposed the natural wood siding on the farmhouse. Weeds and other plants hid a multitude of the property's sins. Topping off the scene of abandonment, a scrawny teenager not much older than fourteen glared at us from the grass alongside the driveway. A buck knife hung out of a hole in his back pocket. His black hair drooped over his eyes, and he weighed a couple of meals short.

From the phone calls I'd had with the owners of the property, I assumed this was the grandchild they'd mentioned, Lucas. The kid's grandfather came out to meet us by the barn.

Fin climbed out of the truck and scanned for threats. He was still skittish despite almost a full year of quiet living. Can't say I blamed him. I was, too. I carried Pa's shotgun everywhere I could. The Wicked Legion weren't all dead, and I was done being stupid.

"I'm Betty Jo." I stuck out a hand to greet him. "We talked on the phone, Mr. Abbott. Is that right?"

"Nice to meet you. Call me John." He shook Fin's hand right after mine, and we were all introduced properly. "I suppose you'd like to look around. Did you want to start at the house or the barns?"

"The barns," I said before Fin could get a word in edgewise. My man knew something was up. But he hid it well. Only a single, "What the heck are you doing?" silent question squinted my way.

We wound around the property, John pointing out the highlights. The tour ended in the barn closest to the house. It was the one that had caught my eye in the first place.

"This one I've been storing parts in. Makes a good machine shed. Used to be a smithy until 1900. Probably needs a lot of work. There's also a shed row barn and the corn crib, but they should get torn down. The mice got into them something awful over the years."

As he talked, I pointed to a small nail jutting out above the wide door. Fin looked up, and his attention fixed on the rough-hewn horseshoe hanging there.

"How old is this farm?" he asked.

John squinted as he thought. "Reckon it was first settled around 1790. This shed was added in 1835. The farmhouse is newer. Granddad got one of them Sears kits in 1916. I was born eight years later, right in that upstairs bedroom." He pointed at the simple white farmhouse. I sneaked a glance at Fin to get a gauge on his reactions, but he wasn't giving me anything.

Then he locked on something in the pile of junk. "Is that an Indian?"

For a rusted heap of motorcycle parts, I knew why it caught his eye. From the beginning of motorcycle history through the Second World War, Harley and Indian fought to dominate the racing scene. Early models, like the one in the corner, set speed records of over a hundred miles per hour. Practically nothing in today's world, but do that on a 50-degree-angled splinter-ridden wooden track riding a rattling bucket of rubber and iron like that old machine, and you're courting death with every race. My Pa used to joke those old bikes had two speeds, "Go, and Go Faster."

John laughed, sharing a knowing smile with Fin. "Hell, yeah. Dad raced her in Woodbridge before they shut the track down."

"Board track?" Fin asked. They both sidled closer to the rusted bike to talk shop, and that was all it took. I knew he was in love.

Over an hour later, the paperwork was signed, and my bank account was emptied. John handed off the keys and wished us well. Then he limped across the street to one of the ranch homes in the subdivision.

Fin stared at the keyring in his hand. "How'd you pay for this?"

"The bank finally closed the accounts, and the garage got sold."

He grunted, a little too speechless for words. That was okay. I'd done my job well. Keeping it a surprise but leaving the final decision to him. I didn't give him much room to wiggle out of it, though. He knew we needed a bigger place. And I knew he missed being able to hammer every day.

The kid who eyeballed us earlier was back.

Fin leaned in and whispered, "I don't like the look of that one."

"That's their grandkid, Lucas. Be nice."

"Snakey little shit." He commented as the kid slipped away with no noise and barely any movement to give him away.

"Takes one to know one," I commented as I went inside the farmhouse to figure out which room I wanted to put my brand-new sewing machine in. There were four big rooms downstairs and three upstairs, plus an attic storage room in the eaves above the kitchen. It was almost too much space for the two of us.

I stood in the middle of the kitchen, which was about as old as the house, and sighed.

"Regretting it already?" Fin came up behind me and rubbed my neck.

"No. I just don't know what to do with this space. You'd have to lug all the groceries through the house or park on the street and tromp through the grass. I think we need to reverse the layout or put parking out front. And I don't want to do that." I'd lived my fill of looking out my front window at a parking lot. I wanted a house that looked like a home, not a damn garage.

"Make it a bar."

"What?"

"This area. Seating over there, and more in the middle room, a bar along that wall. You can store the half barrels in the pantry. Then convert the parlor into the kitchen."

I stared at him. "Who would drink at this bar?"

He rubbed his neck, turning just a little red from embarrassment. Then mumbled something.

"What's that?"

"I said I might invite the local boys over. Seeing as we owe them."

I didn't know any such thing. The local boys were a bunch of rednecks on bikes. The whole lot of them served as a feeder club for the Destroyers chapter northeast of here. "I thought they owed you?" And Big Mike, of course. I tacked that on.

"Well… we kind of commandeered the cabin from them. And they've been running prospects by every weekend to check on us since we arrived. Old Hoss is thorough."

That's why I always heard Harley pipes. Hoss, the president, seemed nice. He wasn't rude to me, at least. "Well, now they can come party, check in on us, and we've got a place to do it at." I stretched my arms out, showing off the space.

A slow smile grew on Fin's face. He walked around and checked all the nooks and crannies. Every so often, he made comments on what needed to be fixed or changed. And as he did, I pictured the place evolving into everything both of us wanted.

Upstairs, he picked the bedroom. There were two more, and one would be perfect as a craft room. The other we could do up as a guest bedroom, since it had the smallest closet I'd ever seen.

He took my hand and led me back downstairs. Every once in a while, he'd bring it to his lips and kiss it.

I'd done good.

"Blenders."

"What?" Fin lifted his head from his inspection of an old radiator.

We were back in the old kitchen we planned to rip out. "I need at least two blenders. Not everyone is going to agree on what they want to drink."

"A beer tap will be just fine. Bikers don't drink the fancy shit like you do."

I held up a finger. "But their old ladies do."

His mouth made a little 'oh' of surprise. "You gonna bring a bunch of bitches into my house?"

"Excuse me? My house. And don't call them bitches. That's not nice." I should know.

"Women." The way he said it almost sounded worse.

"Yes. Women. Old ladies, girlfriends…"

"Strippers?"

"Finnigan Curty!"

He laughed at me getting all riled up. "If there's strippers, I promise not to look much."

"You sound like Ant."

His laughter stopped short. We'd grieved a lot in the last year. Despite that, the corner of his mouth curled up, and he took another look around. "He'd have liked this place. But I'm kind of glad I don't have to deal with his bullshit. Or run interference on him anymore. He was such a flirt."

That little smile fell. I wrapped myself around him and held tight. "You can mount his knife in the barn, next to the horseshoe."

Fin shook his head. "Can't. I'm supposed to bury it with his ashes."

"Where?" We'd taken his ashes with us when we left. A few times along the ride, I thought Fin would pop it open and spread his remains over the scenery, especially in Sturgis. But he never did. Instead, he kept them close.

Fin shrugged. "Anywhere, I guess. I suppose we could be all legal and shit and stick him in a cemetery somewhere, but he'd hate that."

"The barn. Put his urn in the barn. Hell, put it up on a shelf and mount the knife with it."

It was like the sun came out. Fin smiled for real this time. "I'll park that old Indian next to the wall, and mount his urn, knife, and patch over it. God, he'd love that."

That way, you can talk to him every day, too. I didn't say it, but I knew Fin would. "Sounds perfect."

"Like you. Thank you." He tugged me close and kissed me like he'd never stop. His hand went under my shirt, tugging my bra aside so he could finger my tit when I smelled smoke.

Not just any smoke—I smelled pot. "Is that smoke?"

Fin smelled it, too, and made a sour face. "Ten-to-one, it's that little snake."

I wasn't going to take him up on that bet. "I told you, his name is Lucas. Let's go look; make sure it isn't the barn."

It wasn't.

We followed the telltale smell of skunk weed through an overgrown garden to the trees just beyond.

Sure as shit, Lucas was in a treehouse. Stoned as fuck.

He didn't even startle when we caught him.

"Don't you have somewhere to be?" I asked. Like home?

Lucas shrugged and took another long hit. His single-word answer came out strangled as he held his breath. "Nope." He sipped in a little more oxygen to keep the smoke in longer.

Fin put on his show voice and tried to be nice like I asked. "You realize this is our house and land as of this afternoon."

"No, it's not." The kid stuck out a belligerent jaw at Fin.

"Whose is it then?" I asked, testing his assumptions.

"Mine."

"That's some ripe bullshit," Fin muttered. I jabbed him in the ribs with my elbow for swearing around a kid.

"It will be someday," the kid fired back.

"Someday ain't today. You look smart enough to know that."

I kept my mouth shut because Fin was right to set boundaries.

Lucas's scowl spoke volumes. I glanced at Fin with a question communicated by a lifted eyebrow. Hopefully, he caught onto my meaning. This kid needed someone like Fin needed Ant.

He didn't agree with me one hundred percent if the shake of his head was any indication. "Your grandparents are looking for you," Fin said.

"Doubt it. They don't give a fuck. No one gives a fuck about me." He sucked in another deep hit.

Whoa. There was some serious emotional shit going on there. His sour face and the unmistakable angry scowl only teenagers can perfect broadcast his feelings. I might not be the most motherly of women, but this kid needed someone in his corner. Maybe a lot of someones.

I turned my head to see what was going through my man's mind. But his hair hid his face.

Fin stared at his shoes for a minute. It didn't take a rocket scientist to know he was thinking about himself and Ant. Finally, he cleared his throat and asked, "Do you like motorcycles?"

The kid's eyes lit up.

Score.

"Good. 'Got an Indian I need cleaned up. If you're going to trespass on my property, you're going to work. If you don't wanna work, get your ass off. Understood? And don't go sneaking around the house. Betty Jo here will shoot you. She's itching to use her Pa's shotgun, ya hear?"

Somehow, we'd just adopted trouble.

Ant was probably laughing his ass off from the beyond.

To quote from one of my favorite movies, the end is only the beginning...

If you're like me, you want more...
[Looks around, puts a finger on her lips...]
Tell you what, go to this super-secret web page to read a bonus scene.
You may be asked to sign up for a newsletter there. If you do subscribe
you will get two emails a month with what's coming next, freebie links,
and other great content, but you can unsubscribe at ANY time.
shh...

https://caliawilde.com/sneak-peek-of-biker-queen/
The password is: Queen

Did you walk into this universe here?
The Hagerstown series starts with:
Down in Blood by Calia Wilde

Thank you for reading!

ABOUT THE AUTHOR:

Calia Wilde believes the hero isn't always the good guy. She believes some heroes and heroines cannot play by the rules to get their happily ever after.

She is a writer of misfits, anti-heroes, villains, underdogs, fringe elements, and other tropes that will likely get her barred from polite society.

As a feral Gen-Xer, she spent numerous hours roaming the woods in search of elves, fairies, or anything that would take her away from the dreaded curse of doing dishes. She once fell off a wardrobe, but instead of landing in Narnia, a very emphatic order of *"Don't tell Mom,"* was decreed. In case you are wondering, yes, she did land on her head.

One time in Sturgis, she was offered twenty bucks to climb a ladder. She declined as there was some fine print regarding the quest that went beyond conquering a fear of heights and some activities which were definitely illegal for someone her age. But it was there... in that magical realm of bikers, booze, and foul language, that she came into the possession of her very first item of armor... aka, black clothing. The forbidden was in her grasp and became an life-long obsession to avoid anything pastel.

As she searched for a career that would indulge this penchant for wearing black, she stumbled upon the world of special effects and excitedly pursued the art of sleeping in strange hotels, working ungodly hours, and handling anything that could, and would, burn, blind, explode, freeze, or otherwise entertain wildlings like herself.

Her current fictional worlds are forged in a hippie world where music and nature peacefully co-exist away from modern conveniences, like bathtubs. Okay, there's a shower, but she has to share it with spiders. Yuck. Which is why she looks forward to going on the road once more where the hotel may have a real tub. Or a hot tub... maybe a heated pool... please?

So, she BEGS you to leave a review and do a good deed by encouraging others to read her books. With enough fans scattered across the globe, she'll have to travel, right? Then she'll have an excuse to leave the farm.

Want a FREE BOOK? Sign up for her newsletter.
CaliaWilde.com/newsletter-sign-up/

or

Become an ARC reader and get all the books FIRST.
CaliaWilde.com/become-an-arc-reader/

Walk on the Wilde side here:
CaliaWilde.com

www.ingramcontent.com/pod-product-compliance
Lightning Source LLC
Chambersburg PA
CBHW020106180626
46812CB00006B/2490